Spring Tide

by the same author
STANDING LIONS

SPRING TIDE

MARY RAY

illustrated by
JANET DUCHESNE

FABER AND FABER
24 Russell Square
London

First published in 1969
by Faber and Faber Limited
24 Russell Square London WC1
Printed in Great Britain
by The Bowering Press Plymouth

SBN 571 08397 8

Contents

1

Deisi!

The clear sun of the first warm afternoon in spring shone down on the small wood growing along the crest of the hill above the estuary. Con walked carefully up the narrow, sun-splashed path that led to the smaller clearing at the northern end; he was pleasantly stiff after a morning cutting beansticks, and now he was trying to make as little noise as possible, because his friend Julius, whom he had missed some time before, was probably just ahead, watching the hole that might be a fox's earth.

Con saw him from the top of a bank through the thin cover where the leaves of the young beech trees were just beginning to split into fans of transparent green. Julius was lying behind a buttress of roots from the great oak tree, his cloak spread among the windflowers. It had rained the night before and the damp would have soaked through by now, but he had probably not noticed it.

He rolled over and sat up as Con scrambled down the bank towards him. He was a red-haired boy with a thin face and brown eyes. Con, a little older and fair, had the square-set Roman bones that were unusual in this far-western province of the Empire.

"Did you see anything?" Con asked, and then, not waiting for an answer, "Julius, I think there's a new warren up on the far side of the hill. Fabius says he'll bring us up here one night and show us how he used to set snares when he was a boy!"

"Oh, good. Is it time to move?"

"Yes, if we're to get the last of the wood loaded and be back in Caer Taff before dusk. The days are still short. Up you come!"

He pulled Julius to his feet; they were the same height almost, though Con was wider across the shoulders. Caer Taff, the fort and the small town around it that was their home, lay behind them now, hidden by the hillside and the trees that grew in the long valley that sloped up from the river and the wharfs on the seaward side.

Up among the trees there was the sound of an axe, and the creaking and muffled thud of a falling tree.

Julius smiled. "Fabius will be stiff tonight; I shouldn't think he's used an axe like that since last autumn!"

"No, but we are supposed to be helping him," said Con. "Our fathers wouldn't have let us spend the day up here without him, so we'd better go and pay for our holiday before we go home. Why do you have to like watching things more than doing them?"

"I . . . Con, wait!" But Con was running up the path ahead, and into the clearing.

Two pack-horses were grazing on the far side, where a servant was trimming a pile of saplings into poles and bean-sticks. Close at hand a tall man was resting on his axe, Caius Fabius Aemilius, architect and builder. He smiled when he saw them and pushed the untidy dark hair back from his face, leaving a green smear across his forehead.

"Good! Julius, it's your turn now. I think I've done my share, and my stiff arm's had enough. Another hour and then we must pack up. I wonder where Lavinia has got to?"

"Shall I find her, sir?" asked Con.

"Oh no, you can help me cord this lot first!" said the man. "She won't have gone far, she's sensible for eleven."

They worked together till the poles were ready for loading, then they gathered round a blanket that had been spread on the grass with the last of an earlier meal.

"Thirsty?" asked Fabius, passing over a leather jug.

Con drank and then wandered across to a break in the trees; the road, that ran west from the bridges below the fort, curved across a stretch of open ground beyond the hillside. There was seldom much to be seen on it except on market day, and now it was empty except for two travellers some way off. It was too far to see clearly but they seemed to be a young man walking and an older riding a mule. Suddenly, while he watched, Con saw the younger man run to the animal's head and pull it to one side of the road; then he saw why. A horse being ridden hard burst out from the woods on the far side of the valley, galloping east towards Caer Taff. He could imagine what the old man was saying now as he shook the mud thrown up by the flying hooves from his cloak, yet Con half-thought the horse had checked for a moment as it passed the two travellers.

He turned back to the others. "That's strange, I've just seen what looked like a post-horse on the road, and whoever sent the message was in a hurry."

"A horse ridden fast?" asked Fabius. "Let me see."

"You're too late," said Con, as the man joined him. "Wait a minute, though. Before it passed those two were going west, now they've turned round and they're coming this way as fast as they can. Look, the man's running!"

"Get the horses loaded, Publius. No, leave the wood, we can fetch it later." Fabius's voice was suddenly harsh, and Con, turning in surprise, saw that his face had changed.

"What is it?"

Before he answered the man turned and called, "Vinny, come back now, Vinny."

"Shall I go for her?" asked Julius.

"No, wait a minute, I want to tell you something before she gets back. I hope I may be wrong and I don't want to frighten her. What you saw, Con, looks to me like bad news from further west, news that isn't unexpected either; and those two with the mule must have been upset by it. Look, they're out of sight already."

"I think I see," said Con, his face serious. "You mean it's the Deisi again; but it was quiet last year, they didn't raid this way at all."

"Maybe not, but there are some people who think that was only because they were gathering strength in Hivernia, and that this year they'll mean business. Your father does for one, Con, and he picks up more gossip of that sort in the mess than I do at the bath-house. I should have thought of this before I brought you two up here, but it's been quiet so long."

"Look, here's Vinny," said Julius.

The daughter of Fabius the architect was a thin child with her father's dark hair, that was flying out from under her scarf now as if she had been running; she came into the clearing, her russet tunic held high, with a puzzled look on her face.

"Quickly, Vinny, we're going now," said her father. "Pack up those primrose roots of yours."

But Lavinia did not obey him at once, she stood looking worried. "Father, I saw something strange down on the far side of the wood."

Fabius paused, still bending over the horse panier he was strapping. "How was it strange, Vinny?" His voice was quiet and steady.

"You know where the trees stop and it slopes down to the stream? I think there were men in the fir plantation behind, and they were hiding."

"Vinny, if they were hiding how could you see they were men? Perhaps it was some of the cavalry horses grazing further away from the fort than usual," said Julius.

"With all their harness on? I saw the sun flashing on something made of metal. It could have been a helmet, and the bushes were moving in several places."

Julius opened his mouth and then shut it again; he looked at Fabius.

"Let's be quite clear," said the architect. "Where were you standing when you saw all this?"

"On the edge of the wood: I don't think anyone would have seen me. Whoever was there had disturbed some pigeons and I thought it was strange, so I went carefully."

Fabius looked relieved. "That was sensible of you." He turned to the two boys, and his face was more serious than they had ever seen it before.

"It looks as if my first guess was right. Still, they've never been known to attack in daylight. I think they must be lying up till dusk, so we should have a little time."

"We can get back to the fort then," said Con.

"Perhaps we could, though that's not certain, but we aren't the only people to think about. The Deisi won't attack the fort directly, but there are the farms between here and the river to think about. We can't warn everyone, but I'm thinking of Vericus."

"But there's Vinny," said Con.

"Of course there is. Do you think I haven't remembered her?" Fabius's voice was sharp.

"You don't think it's just possible that we may be wrong, do you?" said Julius quickly. "Couldn't we go and see, sir, while you go ahead to the farm with Vinny?"

"And how could I explain it to your father Septimius if I rode safe into Caer Taff and you were never seen again? Come on now, Vinny, up here between the paniers." He swung her up on to one of the horses. "Publius, you take the other on ahead, you know the way."

"I think Julius is right," said Con unexpectedly. "We're old enough not to do anything stupid, or anyway I shall be old enough to join the Eagles next year. I promise we'll be after you as fast as our legs can carry us when we've had a quick look."

"There isn't time to argue," said Fabius, "I'll have to trust you, only don't think you're a whole legion, Con. You may know these woods, but the Deisi are another sort of experts themselves."

He led the second horse after Publius, with Lavinia perched between the paniers, her small face more puzzled than frightened.

"You go first," said Con. "I think you know this path better than I do. Jupiter! I wish Father was back from Isca. If it is the raiders what can they be doing so near to the fort?"

It was not far back along the path to the edge of the trees. The birds were silent in the late afternoon hush, so that the whole wood had a waiting stillness. Some way short of the hazel bushes at the edge of the trees, Julius stopped.

"We'd better decide what we're going to do," he said quietly.

Con loosened his knife in its sheath and bent to tighten a sandal strap. "If we have a look first from where Vinny saw them, we may see something. If we don't we'd better separate. There's cover most of the way down on the east side of the ridge, isn't there?"

"Yes, there are the fir trees that Vericus planted as a wind-break some years back, but there's no cover the other way."

"What about the stream-bed? Anyway, let's have a look together first."

They went forward even more carefully the last few yards before striking off to the right and crawling under the bushes away from the path. Con parted the stems in front of him and looked down into the valley.

Nothing moved. A little wind rippled the rough grass and a gull glided by high up, its wings motionless. The sun was well down in the sky to the west now and it was beginning to be chilly. Julius half-raised himself to crawl back, but Con stayed him without taking his eyes off the line of undergrowth below them. They lay motionless again.

An ant ran across Con's legs, but he remembered not to knock it off with a jerk. Then Julius drew in his breath and pointed. To their left, already up among the young firs, there were men moving. The undergrowth was still thin in places among the new trees and they saw three figures run across a gap and disappear again.

Con looked the other way, where the stream ran down among rushes to a pond in a clump of elder trees. Even as he watched a bird burst up from among them with a clattering alarm call. He crawled back to the path, followed by Julius.

"It's the Deisi all right, and they're moving already," he whispered. "It's too late to try to get an idea of numbers; we'd better get back as quickly as we can."

They turned back along the path, running as quickly as they could under the low branches. Julius had been frightened when Fabius first spoke about the Deisi, with the sickening jolt of unexpected fear. Since then he had been busy, but now his imagination was working again. He had spent all his life under the shadow of the walls of a Roman fort, and although his father was a merchant, not a soldier like Con's, the lives of everyone in Caer Taff were closely bound up with the rhythms and routines of army life. Scout boats went out from the harbour mouth down river from the fort, and did not always come back; in the last few years the Deisi had raided west along the coast, and the cohort which had gone to reinforce the local garrisons had not come back unscathed. West Britain was an outpost on the frontiers of the Empire, yet when year after year you lived peacefully in the same place, and there was food in the market, and you never saw barn roofs go up in flames, you did not understand that this could be a real part of your life. Now there were armed raiders within hailing distance behind him, and for the first time he knew in the pit of his stomach that before sunset he might have been wounded himself, or, what was more horrible, have seen people hurt that he knew and was fond of. He remembered Vinny, and then he shut that part of his mind firmly and began trying to find the quickest short cut among the trees on the slopes above Vericus's farm.

Con, as he followed behind, was not thinking about himself, his mind was ahead at the farm trying to picture it, and wondering how easy it would be to defend. Fabius would have got a messenger away down to the fort as soon as he arrived, and if he was well mounted he should get through all right and they could expect help not long after dusk. He hoped that Fabius would have started to move wagons across the front courtyard by the time he got there, but he was a civilian architect, not a centurion, and might not see the best ways of making the farm defensible. Then he remembered that Vericus who now owned the farm was a retired veteran, and the ex-standard bearer of the third cohort at that, and he realised that whoever directed the siege it was not likely to be himself.

The woods were quiet and they met no one until they reached the field at the back of the farm, but from there they could see that it hummed with activity. The last of the cattle were being driven through the gateway at the side that led into the kitchen courtyard. Ahead lay the main hall of the farm with rooms projecting on each side; they heard the voice of Vericus coming from the open space in front of the main door.

"Thank the Gods!" he shouted when he saw them. He was a big man with a voice to match. "I was going to send some men back to look for you. It was a fool's trick scouting on your own, and I wouldn't have liked to answer to the Centurion for you."

"I didn't think they'd be moving yet, but they are," said Con. "We saw them just now up among the fir trees."

"There's no doubt then?" said Fabius, coming towards them.

"No," said Con. "Even if it isn't the Deisi, they're fighting men and not Romans. We saw three plainly and they had helmets and spears, but it was too far away for anything else."

Vericus looked round grimly at the muddy courtyard in front of the hall. It was protected on two sides by the short projecting wings, which housed a bath-house and store-rooms, but ahead there was only a light fence that would do no more than keep out stray cattle.

"I was meaning to get a wall built across there this summer, and now we're caught unready." He went to the gateway and shouted, "Hurry up with those wagons," and then stumped through it, lame in one leg and leaning on a stick the size of Hercules's club. Con and Julius looked quickly at each other, and then ran after him.

2

Bean Soup

In another half hour there was not much more that anyone could do except wait, and that was not likely to be for long. The farm boy, who had been sent off earlier on the best horse, had not returned and they could only hope he had reached the bridge safely. Vericus and Fabius collected everyone in the kitchen yard, and they were pitifully few in number—one farm-hand and Publius, who were both too elderly to be much use, a boy, and the cook—a woman with the shoulders of a champion wrestler, who seemed likely to be as useful as any man.

"Five men with the one who's back scouting in the woods, and three boys!" said Vericus. "I suppose they knew that this was Beltane Night and all the men who could walk that far would be down in the town getting drunk. Caius Fabius, will your little girl do what she's told?"

"Oh yes, Lavinia's fairly sensible. She'll be as scared as anyone but she won't be a nuisance."

"She'll be safest in the kitchen with the farm girls. Elyned knows the way into the ice-room under the store; if things don't go well they should be safe down there till the army gets here. The raiders won't find it straight away, and if they should, Elyned knows what to do."

The boys stood a little way away talking quietly. They

each had a short sword now, as well as their own knives, and Julius had a leather hunting cap from Vericus's arms-chest, that had fitted him better than Con.

"It can't be long now," he said.

"We should get a little warning from the man in the woods."

"Con," called Fabius, "you can get on to the roof of the west wing through the hall; take old Publius with you, he's handy with a bow and he'll have a good line of fire each way."

"What shall I do?" asked Julius.

"Stay here," said Vericus. "There's no point in spreading ourselves too thinly. The side gate's important but we're weakest at the front of the hall; those wagons won't keep anyone out for more than a few minutes. We haven't got more than half a chance if it's a full raiding party and they mean business. But they probably don't know we're expecting them, so any defence will give them something to think about."

Con grinned a little lopsidedly at Julius. "So we're in our first fight together, I never expected that. Good luck!" He went through into the hall with old Publius behind him.

After that it was very quiet. Con climbed the ladder that led to the flat roof above the store-rooms. There was a low parapet along two sides, and the higher roof of the main building gave some cover. Below to his right was the open space behind the front gate, Vericus had his two wagons drawn up inside the wattle fence, and he could see him behind them, with Fabius and the farm boy. Behind them the door of the bath-house had been left swinging, and a blanket dropped by one of the maids when the more valuable stores were taken into the hall, was lying on the path. He wanted to go down and shut the door, but neither of the men below had noticed it as they watched the open clearing in front of the farm. It was laid out in two small barley fields, with the green shoots bright and clean after the rain of the day before.

A shout came from the side of the house. That was where Julius was. With any luck the man that Vericus had sent out to scout was coming back. There was more shouting; if only he could see what was happening. Then Publius touched his arm and pointed. There was something moving on the main path between the barley fields.

Publius fitted an arrow to his bow as he crouched behind the parapet. The low rays of the sun, striking almost level across the clearing ahead, made it difficult to see clearly.

Publius raised his bow, taking aim, but Con knocked down his arm. "No, wait a minute."

It was no Deisi raider who had broken through the trees but a young man, running with his head down, and behind him a weary mule that was making what speed it could. It looked as if it had been a poor animal to start with, but the man on its back seemed in no better condition, he was bouncing and shaking like a sack of grain—as if he had very little control over where he was going. Half-way across the open space his companion stopped and turned. There was shouting behind in the trees, and the rider dug his heels again into the mule's flanks, but it could go no faster. Then a black spear hissed from the bushes; it bucked, its front legs gave way, and it rolled over.

The rider fell clear, but he lay without moving till the younger man ran back. Another spear flashed as the Deisi broke cover, but he ran on, straight towards them. He had barely time to swing his companion over his shoulder and turn back towards the farm when the first of the raiders was up with him. Then Publius's bow twanged, and the attacker fell back, tugging at an arrow in his shoulder.

BEAN SOUP

It was only a few steps more. Vericus had the gate open ready as the young man tottered through.

"Into the hall with him," he shouted.

Con thought the young man would let his companion slip to the ground before he reached the door, but he seemed strongly built, although it was difficult to tell his height from above. All Con could see was a head of startlingly red hair; Julius's was bright enough, but this was something altogether different.

Then Publius shouted and shot again, and Con turned back to his post. The Deisi had scattered when their leader was wounded. Now they were strung across the clearing, eight or nine men in shaggy tattered garments with horned helmets, dark and savage-looking, shouting horribly. The next arrow took one in the leg and he began to crawl back out of the clearing, but the others ran on, trampling through the young barley. Con heard someone screaming over on the other side of the building, they must be attacking all round. His mouth felt suddenly dry but there did not seem time to be frightened. Then he realised for the first time that unless the attackers actually tried to scale the wall below him he had no weapon to use against them. His sword would be no use up here. He saw a pile of broken roofing tiles in one corner; they were too heavy to throw far, but he would damage anyone he did hit.

Publius's next shot missed and now they were below him, running up the side of the building and within his range. There was no time to look to the right and see what was happening round the wagons.

He threw at the leader, aiming for his head, but the tile took him on the shoulder, a glancing blow. Con threw again, judging the time better as the man ran forward with his head bent. The blow fell on the back of his neck and he

26

keeled over, his leather helmet rolling away under the feet of those who followed him.

But now there were more men under the trees. Con, turning back for more tiles, ducked as an arrow whistled close above his head. There were several archers firing from shelter. Another came that trailed a plume of smoke; it fell behind him and burnt harmlessly on the dusty tiles. Then one snaked into the thatch that sloped above the last of the store-rooms and it began to blaze furiously. Con and the old man were driven back, choking in the smoke.

Near the wall of the hall the air was clearer. "Stay up here as long as you can!" Con shouted above the noise of the flames. There seemed to be smoke in the courtyard as well, it looked as if one of the wagons was on fire. He ran down the stairs, there was no more he could do up there.

Below in the hall smoke was pouring through the doorway that led to the store-rooms, and he heard the sound of feeble coughing. An old man lay across the doorway. Although he was slightly built he was heavy to drag; when Con had him clear of the smoke he saw that it must be the stranger who had fallen off the mule. He looked as if he was dying, his face leaden and a thin dribble coming from the corner of his mouth; Con did not dare to leave him until he was propped against a pile of blankets, thrown down where the door to the kitchen yard made a cross draught. Just as he was turning back towards the store-room, the old man coughed again and opened his eyes.

"It was the oil jars," he whispered. "I saw them from the doorway and I tried to douse the fire, but I couldn't . . ."

Con did not wait to hear more, he pulled the top blanket from the pile and ran back towards the store-rooms.

*　　*　　*　　*

BEAN SOUP

Julius coughed as smoke from something burning on the other side of the house drifted across the courtyard. A couple of arrows clattered harmlessly behind him on the worn paving stones, and the cattle crowded into the stables lowed uneasily.

Vericus emerged from the hall for a moment to shout, "Julius, get close under the wall," then there was a piercing scream from the north gateway and he disappeared. He was alone now with the cook and the old farm-hand. Still, the cook had a meat axe and looked businesslike.

The gate began to shiver under the blows of axes from outside. "Come on," he shouted to her. "We'll have to try to keep them out. That gate won't last long, but they can't get through many at a time."

The middle plank gave way and an arm came through, reaching for the beam. Julius slashed at it with his sword. The blow landed partly on the wood but the arm disappeared. The axe blows began again. Almost at once the leather hinges gave way and the door fell inwards in one piece. The two men who climbed through looked enormous in the fading light. The cook jumped forward, her axe held high, shouting some Silurian war-cry half-remembered from her grandfather; Julius shouted too and leapt after her.

It was only because he had space to fight in that he survived, for the raiders were still confined in the gateway. The leader made a tremendous swipe with the axe he was still holding. Julius ducked and then struck in under his guard as the great hairy, sweating, half-naked man before him stumbled over the wreckage of the door. The point of his sword went in somewhere among the folds of the skin tunic, but as the man fell he was pulled back out of the way by those behind him. Julius glanced to his left, he had not seen how the cook had fared but she was still on her feet, panting, with the sweat running down her fat cheeks and blood on the blade of her chopper.

The attack began again. Julius knew he could not resist these trained warriors for long. He was no fighting man himself, already his sword arm was tiring. If only Con was here with him!

There was a warning shout from his left and he jumped back as the old man tumbled an enormous bale of hay across the broken doorway. For a moment the attackers checked, then, as the first jumped across it, a flaming brand fell on to the dry grass and it flared up in his face.

Julius saw the old man dancing and grinning like a satyr. For a moment they were safe. He drew back from the fierce heat, all at once very tired. The cook was cleaning her axe.

"First blood to us!" she called.

Julius could not think of an answer to that which the woman would understand, only something about Amazons that wasn't suitable. He wondered what was happening to Con and Fabius, and if Lavinia was very frightened; she had been very quiet when he saw her just before the battle started and it was hard to tell with children. O God, the flames were dying down. Water swooshed on them from the other side of the gate, and they went up in a hissing cloud of steam.

"This is it!" thought Julius. "The next man through that gate is going to kill me. Then perhaps it will all be over and the others will be all right. Please let this be a dream and let me wake up now."

Then, after the way of dreams, something quite unreasonable happened. Just as a dark, skinny man appeared in the gateway and kicked aside the smouldering hay, a small fantastic figure pushed past Julius, staggering under the weight of a large cooking pot. The raider, his eyes on Julius, lunged forward, and in that moment the little figure gave an enormous heave and threw the contents of the pot in his face.

There was shouting behind him and Julius was pushed to one side as Fabius jumped past and pulled the pot-thrower back into safety. Then all at once there were no men in the gateway. A cow-horn was blowing up in the woods, and above it, blessed promise of order and safety, the sound of a Roman trumpet.

Julius turned slowly back into the courtyard; Fabius was kneeling in the middle, blood oozing from a slash across his forehead, his arms tight round Lavinia.

"It was you?" said Julius stupidly.

Lavinia looked at him speechlessly over her father's shoulder and burst into tears. Her face was dirty, and tied over her tunic was the cook's leather butchering apron, covering her from neck to ankles like a great shield.

"But what did she throw?" asked Julius.

The cook bent and sniffed the dregs in the pot. "Bean soup, it holds the heat. There'll be a scalded pirate down there in the woods somewhere!" She cackled with laughter.

A detail of legionaries ran past the ruined gateway and a centurion on a chestnut horse reined up and jumped down. He strode through into the courtyard, flinging the great white cloak back from his shoulders.

"Why Fabius, are you here?" he shouted. "Can you tell me what happened, is anyone hurt?"

Fabius got up slowly from his knees, an arm still round his daughter. "Cousin Aemilius," he said, "I don't think I've ever been so glad to see anyone."

Vericus came through from the hall, followed by a strange

young man with red hair. "So the Gods of Rome still listen occasionally," he roared. "Ten more minutes, sir, and you could have saved yourself the pains."

"Is anybody hurt?" asked the centurion again. "Fabius, that's a nasty cut on your head. You should have it seen to at once."

Vericus looked around him. "We lost a lad by the other gate, he got an arrow in his neck, but your own boy should be here somewhere."

"Con here? Then where is he?"

"Father!" Con came slowly through the door from the main hall. His hair was singed and the front of his tunic charred and crumbling. He had wrapped a rag about his right forearm and stood there fumbling with it.

The centurion crossed the yard in three strides and took his son by the shoulders. "Con, if I'd known you were here . . . are you hurt?"

"Not really. A burning arrow caught the roof of one of the store-rooms, it was the one with the oil jars, and I've been putting the fire out."

"When did you get back?" asked Fabius. "I thought you were still at Isca."

"Only an hour ago. I was at the Praetorium when your messenger rode in. I know the ground well, so the Prefect sent me up in command. It's the men of Vericus's old Century down there in the woods now."

There was a pause; suddenly there was no more to say. It was too early to start to piece together the story of what had happened, and now that the attack was over everyone was suddenly too tired to start to count the cost and begin clearing up the mess that the raiders had left behind them. Then the cook appeared in the kitchen doorway, followed by a girl carrying a tray of cups.

"That fighting was hot work," she said amiably. "I hoped you wouldn't mind me opening a new jar, sir!"

Julius let out a crow of laughter that was almost a sob. "You sound as if this was a dinner party!"

"Julius!" Con took a step towards him. Then his legs gave way. Aemilius caught him as he fell, and with his son in his arms strode through the dusk into the main hall.

3

A Young Man with Red Hair

"Steady," said an unfamiliar voice, swimming out of what felt like a ringing emptiness inside Con's head.

His right arm, which had been part of the general feeling of being uncomfortable, suddenly began to hurt quite badly. Con grunted and tried to sit up.

"Hold on just a minute longer, I've nearly finished," said the voice, and a firm hand pressed him back.

Con opened his eyes. He was lying on his back in what seemed to be a very large and badly lit hall; then he realised that he was lying on a mattress on the floor and that someone's head was blotting out most of the light. It was a young man with a square face, the eyes deep set under strong brows, and Con could not remember ever having seen him before. Then he saw the hair, deep red, edged now like flame by the lamp behind, and he remembered the two strangers who had come in from the woods, and the flames that had licked across the straw-covered wine jars towards the oil store. The wooden shelves had collapsed and hit him on the head.

The young man finished bandaging the arm and smiled down at him. "Is that too tight? I thought if I was quick I'd get it finished before you came to."

"It's not bad, is it?" asked Con. His arm was hurting now, but he could not remember much about burning it.

"No, it should heal in ten days, only you'd got some dirt in it and I had to get it clean. Now there's just a little scorching on your chest, when your friend comes with some clean water."

He bent over and undid Con's tunic at the neck, then he shook his head. "No, I'll have to cut this or I won't get it down you; anyway your mother will have to put a fresh front on, it's too burnt to take a patch." Julius knelt beside him and put down a bowl of water, he looked worried and rather white.

"Please, who are you?" Con asked, as the young man began to clean the shallow burn on his chest.

"Of course, I must be rather unexpected!" The young man laughed. "My name is Brychan, and my friend whom you towed out of the way of the fire is Amphibalus. We were on the road west to kinfolk of mine at Nidum, but as you can see we judged the day badly. Julius, is there some oil left? Will you hold the bottle?"

Although the pain was not so bad this time the burn was bigger and Con found it very hard to keep still. "Is your friend all right?" he asked through his teeth. "He looked very ill. No, I'm not dying, Julius, but it does sting."

"Sit up while I get the bandage round you," said Brychan. "I'm afraid my friend is far from well, we've been a long time on our journey already and he was beginning to be troubled by an old sickness before today. I hoped that if we pushed on we could reach our friends and he would recover there. He's not in much pain now but this afternoon's alarm has weakened him. I shall have to find somewhere for him to rest for a few days before we go on."

"The road to Nidum won't be clear for a while anyway, after the raid," said Julius.

"No, of course, I hadn't had time to realise that." Some-

34

thing, the shadow of some deeper concern, showed for a moment in his eyes.

Con began to wonder who he was. At a distance, from the colour of his hair, he could almost have been taken for one of the local Silurian tribesmen, though that could be said of other people in Caer Taff including Julius. He did not talk like a tribesman, and yet he had not quite the accent of a good garrison school. For the moment it would not be polite to ask questions, but perhaps Julius had heard more than he had.

"There, that will do for tonight," Brychan smiled a strangely reassuring smile, and then paused to give him that slightly lengthened look that he remembered from his mother when he was small and not well. He seemed satisfied, gathered up the bowl and towel he had been using, and moved out of sight.

Tables were being put up now, and the maids were laying them with bowls and cups; a bitter smell of burning still hung in the hall. Vericus and Fabius came through the thick curtain that had been drawn across the main doorway, bringing with them a scatter of raindrops and a draught of cool night air to flatten the lamp-flames.

"All's as well as it can be tonight," said Vericus. "We've been round and made sure all the fires are out. Tomorrow in daylight we shall be able to take stock of the damage."

Aemilius came in after them, undoing his great cloak, darkened over the shoulders with rain. "It's going to be a wet night. It's a good thing you've still got a roof over your head, Vericus. I've set my guard and put the reliefs in your stables."

He came over to Con and went down on one knee beside him. "You look better! I'm glad your mother isn't here, you'd have frightened her to death, fainting like that."

"I know, I do feel silly. It isn't as if I'd been wounded, I could have burnt myself in our own kitchen!"

"You needn't worry, Con. It counts, even if no one stuck a sword in you, as it would if you were thrown during a battle and your horse kicked you!" said Aemilius in an amused voice.

He got up and went back to the other men, who were grouped around the tables now, eating standing up. Julius came over with a steaming bowl and a hunk of bread.

"Do you need any help?"

"No, as long as that doesn't need cutting up. Is it soup?"

Julius laughed. "Not bean soup, anyway, the cook must have been cooking two sorts at once. Oh, I forgot, you don't know about that yet."

While they ate they put together a full account of what had happened during the short minutes of the attack.

Then Julius said, "Con, Fabius told me just now, they've got the bodies of the Deisi and our boy laid out in one of the outhouses."

"How many?"

"We killed four. One of them had a broken neck, I think it must have been the man you hit with a tile."

"He is dead then? I thought he was, only I didn't think about it at the time. It's strange, I've always wanted to follow Father into the legion, ever since I was tiny and we used to play Romans and Parthians, I always expected that I should fight and kill people one day, because soldiers do, only I didn't think I was going to kill a man today when I got up this morning."

Suddenly he realised that if he was not very careful he was going to cry, and he did not want to do that in front of Julius, even if it was only because he was tired and his head ached and his arm was hurting again. He swallowed hard and said, "Anyway, you've been in hand-to-hand fighting before me."

"Don't remind me! Really, it's all been a strange business; most of what's happened seems to be more by luck than organisation. Imagine if the farm horse had gone lame, or your father hadn't been ready to ride at once, or there hadn't been soup cooking for supper. I suppose fighting's always like that."

"The big battles are different," said Con firmly.

"How much of your life are you going to spend fighting them? Still, I'm not going to argue with you when you ought to be asleep, or resting at any rate. I'll pull my mattress over by yours in case you need anything in the night. It's awkward for you with only one hand."

Lavinia came out from the kitchen, where she had been eating supper with her new friend Elyned, one of Vericus's farm girls, and went over to her father, looking puzzled.

"I thought now it was over we would go home. Won't Mother be worried?"

Fabius sat down in Vericus's large carved chair and pulled her on to his knee. "It's like this, sweetheart. Now Uncle Aemilius and his men have come we're quite safe here, but there are still lots of raiders being hunted through the woods, and it's much better for us to keep out of the way till that's over; in the morning we can all go back to Caer Taff safely. Mother won't be expecting us till then because we sent a message back to the Prefect and he will have told her we're safe; and Julius's father as well."

Lavinia looked about her from the security of her father's lap and said, "I see. It's exciting now, isn't it, all sleeping in here as if you were playing a game. What's going to happen to me?"

37

"Elyned will find you a bed in the women's room, so don't make a nuisance of yourself!"

She giggled, and put up a hand to tuck in the end of the bandage round his forehead; Fabius had a habit of not keeping things tidy. "You didn't tell me how this happened."

"Did I not? It was when the boy was killed, darling. We were all crouching behind a cart; then a burning arrow fell into it and set some straw on fire. It ought to have been cleared out before we put the cart there but there wasn't time. Anyway, it meant that we had to run back to the main door, because the smoke was so thick we couldn't see what was happening. That was when the boy was killed."

"Did it hurt him very much?"

"No, I don't think it could have. I came out again as soon as I could, and by then he was already dead and quite quiet. Then one of the Deisi came through the smoke and hit me. I was lucky because he knocked me right out, and when I fell down he didn't bother to see if I was properly dead. The next thing I knew was Brychan trying to pull me back into the house, and because I'd never seen him before I tried to fight him."

Brychan, sitting on a mattress in a corner away from the others, looked up when he heard his name. The old man was lying very still beside him, propped high against a heap of cushions from the dining couches; earlier his eyes had been open, but now he seemed to be asleep. Brychan glanced down at the quiet face of his friend. All seemed well, so he got up and came over to stand beside Fabius's chair.

"I think he'll sleep now, the cook gave me a special draught for him."

"Brychan," said Fabius, "I'm only just beginning to realise that one of the luckiest things that every happened to me was that you were on the Nidum road this afternoon.

I think you saved my life when I was lying there beside the wagon. It was ill fortune for you to be caught up in all this, but thank you. I was a stranger, and I might have been dead already and your courage wasted. No one would have blamed you if you had not come to help me." He put his hand out and laid it for a moment on the younger man's arm.

Brychan had flushed slowly up to the roots of his flame-coloured hair. "Please," he said. "What else could I have done? Anyway, the hall was full of smoke, it was healthier outside!"

Fabius let out a cackle of laughter that made everyone in the hall turn round. "If that's the way you think when things are dangerous you should be in the army; or no, perhaps not, being a civilian can be nearly as perilous in this province."

Elyned came out of the kitchen, her eye on Lavinia. "Please sir," she said, "the young lady should be in bed. Will you come, my love?"

Lavinia slid down obediently from her father's lap; Fabius bent to kiss her goodnight. "Sleep well, there's half a century of legionaries prowling round in the darkness to keep you safe," he said.

Lavinia laughed. "I'm not frightened, though I'm glad they're there. Goodnight, Father." Then she looked around her. "I can't say goodnight to everyone or Elyned will get cross, but please, Brychan, thank you for saving my father; I'm very glad he's still alive and I'm sure Mother is too. Goodnight." She stood on tiptoe and kissed him, and after a moment of surprise he put an arm about her and kissed her back.

After Lavinia had gone the two men looked at each other. "Well," said Fabius, "what my daughter lacks in social experience she makes up for in sincerity, and I don't think I put it much better myself. I suppose we'd all better go to bed, it hasn't been an easy day. Have you a mattress over there, Brychan?"

The young man seemed to have recovered from his embarrassment. "Yes, by Amphibalus, though I don't want to sleep for a little yet. I must make sure he's all right, he has a habit of not waking me if he needs anything in the night, which can be awkward." He looked suddenly tired and troubled.

Fabius dropped his voice so that it did not carry to the other side of the table. "Brychan, can I help you? I think I can understand a little how you feel with your journey interrupted and your friend ill. Now you may have to wait in

Caer Taff for days till it's safe to set out again, and I think there may not be much money to pay for lodgings and a doctor for Amphibalus."

Brychan looked ruefully down at his tunic, which was clean but much patched. "Yes, I was thinking that I must try to find work. I grew up on a farm, on the edge of the hill-country westward; that's a life that makes a man able to turn his hand to most things, and I can write and figure too, Amphibalus taught me. What's worrying me is that I shan't be able to leave him for very long at a time, not till he can do more for himself."

"Then it seems I'm lucky twice over in meeting you," said Fabius. "You won't know, being a stranger to Caer Taff, but my work is the making and mending of buildings. Even out here there is a right and a wrong way of putting up a house, or repairing a bridge, and not everything is done by the army, even if they like to think so. I'm lucky to live in a place where a man is not thought less of for using his own hands to put a thing right."

Brychan laughed suddenly. "I'm sorry, sir, but I saw you for a moment in a toga with a foot of embroidery round it parading up and down in a half-built palace, while a little man ran along behind you dropping architect's plans. It really didn't fit at all."

"No, it wouldn't," said Fabius, smiling. "But, Brychan, that's just the point. My foreman left me last autumn to make his fortune in Londinium or Aquae Sulis and since then my tallies and plans have been in confusion because I've had no time to look after them myself. If you would stay in my house a month with your friend, and spend what time you could on them I should think I was getting much the best of the bargain. Though perhaps you must be in Nidum before that."

Brychan did not seem to be able to answer him at once. The two boys, curled on Con's mattress, turned away so that it would not be too obvious that they had been listening to what was going on.

"I hope he stays," whispered Julius. "We don't see many new people and there's something strange about him."

"Yes, I know what you mean, and he made a good job of my arm just now. I wonder where he's been, and who the old man is, he doesn't seem to be a relation. It's strange."

"Hush!"

"Caius Fabius," said Brychan, "it's sometimes not easy to know how to accept great generosity, but thank you. I'll do my best to see that you don't lose by it; my handwriting is really quite neat though you might not think it to look at the size of my hands. I hope Amphibalus does wake up tonight so I can tell him; he'll sleep better afterwards, for he has a horror of being a burden to anyone."

"Will he be fit to travel in the morning?" asked Fabius, getting up.

"Yes, if he doesn't have another attack. I think he's in no danger now, only very weary."

"One of Aemilius's men got an arrow through his leg, they can both be carried as far as the road, and then taken the rest of the way by wagon."

Vericus came back into the hall; he had washed himself, and brought out a much-creased ceremonial toga from the bottom of a chest; he was a man who respected the older traditions.

"Centurion, gentlemen," he said, "I think it's fitting that we offer thanks to the Gods of Rome who have protected us today." He pulled a fold of the toga over his head and turned to the small shrine close to the hearth.

Aemilius, Fabius, and the old man Publius, who were in

the hall, went to stand behind him, and Julius got up from the floor. Only Brychan hesitated. Con, watching him curiously behind the backs of the others, saw that his hands had clenched. Then a faint sigh came from Amphibalus. Brychan turned quickly and went to kneel beside him, half-hidden by the curtain, and Con could see that he was trembling.

4

Caer Taff

The next morning everything went more slowly than anyone had expected, for although the raiders had been driven off, the woods were still too dangerous for a slow-moving party to make the hour-long journey to the fort without an escort. It was mid-afternoon before the wounded were finally transferred to a wagon on the main road, and at last the bridge over the river came into sight. Con and Lavinia, mounted on the two pack-horses, rode in front of the cart, while Julius walked behind with Brychan. Now that the town was so near Fabius had gone on ahead.

Con reined in his horse as they reached the top of the small hill above the river to wait for the others to catch up. It was a grey day after the sun of the afternoon before and a thin rain was beginning to fall. He pulled his cloak round the bandaged arm and shook the wet hair out of his eyes; last night he had woken every time he turned over, and now he was weary and his legs felt wobbly. Also his arm still hurt most of the time; it was a small pain, but it helped to make him feel tired.

Then the rain eased a little and he looked down towards the bridge, and suddenly he felt a familiar lightening of heart, which was more than the anticipation of comfort and the security of going home.

44

Below the bridge lay the town wharf with a round-bottomed
grain ship and a collection of smaller craft moored among
the sheds and carts that clustered round the quay. Far to the
right was the flat silver streak of the estuary, colourless in
this light, the far shore only a shadow of cloud. Then there
were the woods and a fold of land hiding the lower moorings
before the town began. There were single houses and farm-
steads at first, then the more ordered rows of roofs that edged

the southern road, with the evening smoke beginning to curl
above them. Last of all, northwards, before the woods began
again and the higher ground that tilted up towards the hill
country, lay the fort. Caer Taff—it stood purposeful, square
and planned, among the civilian muddle of the little town
that had grown up around it.

Over the stone walls the long, low barracks and the higher
roofs of the administration block and the officers' quarters
showed plainly. Threads of smoke rose here too from the
cookhouses, and there was a stir of movement from the
guards on the walls and horses being led in. These were the
afternoon things that had been part of him all his life; Con

had been born here, and although next spring he would leave Caer Taff yet they would still be a part of his future as they had formed his past.

From behind came the sound of more than one horse being ridden hard. Con drew his own over to the side of the road, and reached out his good hand to Lavinia's bridle.

The men who passed them were mired to the thigh and their horses had the straining flanks and drooping heads of beasts that have seen how far there is to go and could no longer be kept on their feet by anything else. Con saw now that the guard on the bridge below had been doubled; the riders passed them with a weary shout and turned left along the road on the other side of the river, making for the west gate and headquarters.

"They will have come from Nidum," said Lavinia. "Perhaps there was a raid there too."

"Perhaps there was," said Con casually, urging his horse back on to the road. "Most certainly," he thought to himself, "it looks as if the whole coast is up." For a moment something tightened inside him, small and cold, which was not like anything he had felt during even the worst times the evening before. An ambush, with the fort secure beyond the hill, was one thing; but if the whole province revolted?

Lavinia seemed to be thinking of something else by now. Perhaps she had not understood, or was it just that she did not show what she was feeling?

The two horses clattered over the bridge and along the narrow road between the south wall of the fort and the first of the houses. Caius Fabius lived half-way along. Twilight was coming early to a sky darkened by rain-clouds, and there were already lights in some of the doorways. Lavinia saw her father come out into the road and called to him; he caught hold of her bridle and she slid down into his arms, still clasping the wilted primroses in their basket that she had saved through all the confusion of the afternoon before.

There were quick steps behind them in the atrium and a tall woman with her fair hair piled high on her head came through the doorway. Lavinia slipped loose from her father, leaving the basket in his hands, and the woman's arms caught her very tight. Above the child's head Domina Helena smiled at her husband, though her mouth trembled.

Con dismounted carefully, trying not to bang his arm, and handed the horse over to the waiting Publius. Then he turned back to the wagon, which had just reached the doorway. Brychan was already bending over Amphibalus, lying on the heaped straw in the back.

"I hope he wasn't bumped too badly," said Fabius, coming up behind them. "I told the driver to go steadily."

The old man opened his eyes and smiled wearily. "Oh no, this was one of the more comfortable of my many journeys."

"Caius Fabius, I should have spoken to you about this before. Perhaps there is some dry place in your stockyard where we could live while we stay with you, and not be under your wife's feet," said Brychan, drawing Fabius aside.

"But she was going to get my little son's room ready. It would be much more comfortable for you, and Lesbius would think it was a treat to move upstairs with Lavinia for a few days."

"No, sir, unless there is nowhere else." Brychan's voice was polite but insistent. "It would be better not."

"The room I use for my tallies in the stockyard has a store behind it that's not often used. You would be warm enough there if you really prefer it. Con, would you go in and tell my wife, before she starts making up beds in the house?"

Con went through into the small atrium, with the little fish-pond in the middle. Domina Helena was already moving about in a room on the right-hand side. She straightened up, her arms full of blankets, looking puzzled, when he had delivered his message.

"I suppose they would be quieter in the store-room," she said. "It hadn't occurred to me. Lesbius can be noisy, and the old man may need a lot of rest."

"I think it's really that they want to be private," said Con. "You know how it is, they've been travelling some time; a quiet place to themselves must be what they want more than anything."

Domina Helena began to fold the blankets. "Con, what are they like? I'm curious; my husband has always been a friendly man, but I've never known him take to anyone strange quite so quickly. I understand that he feels grateful to this Brychan, but he's only been in the house now half an hour, and with all the things that I wanted to hear, all he would talk about was this stranger."

"I think you'll understand better when you meet him, Domina Helena," said Con. "Julius explains this sort of thing better than I do, but he is the sort of man one takes to."

They came out into the atrium together just as Amphibalus was carried through the doorway. Domina Helena put the blankets into the arms of her old servant and said, "Take these, Antonia, I'll come in just a minute." Brychan smiled at her, part in greeting, part in thanks, as he passed, walking carefully with the frail old man in his arms. He went through the doorway at the back of the house into the orchard that led to the stockyard.

Julius came through into the atrium, looking for Con. "So that's over. I'm going up to the bath-house, I think my father will be there and I'm filthy, so I'll walk part of the way with you."

The baths were on the north side of the town, near the river; the house of Aemilius stood beyond them.

"Come on then," said Con. "It's not quite sundown yet, let's take the short cut through the fort."

The guard on the south gate passed them in easily. Con was well known, for although his father was no longer a regular officer, since his time in the legion had expired the year before, he was now re-enlisted for special duties. The boys walked between the barrack blocks towards the Praetorium in the middle of the camp. The fort, spread on either side of the road, was seething with life; the guard for the first quarter of the night was about to go on duty, and the watchkeepers were gathering their squads at the ends of the long, low buildings that housed the two cohorts now stationed in the fort. A waft of wood-smoke and the strong man-smell of sweat and leather and latrines hit them as soon as they passed under the entrance tower.

There seemed to be even more activity in the centre of the camp than usual. A knot of officers was waiting outside headquarters, and two dispatch riders cantered past, making for the north and east gates.

"I wonder what's up," said Con. "I wish I dared ask someone, but Father would be furious if I made a nuisance of myself."

"He'll probably tell you tonight."

"Yes, if he isn't off somewhere else already. Father's retirement is more active than most full military service! It wasn't just an isolated raid, was it? I can smell bigger trouble than I remember for a long time."

"It looks like it. The only thing is, Con, I don't think it's just the Deisi. I heard your father talking to Vericus about something else when I was trying to sleep last night."

"You don't mean the whole province is rising, the Silures

as well?" Con stopped dead just in front of the north gate tower.

Julius took him by the arm and steered him through and out on to the road to the bath-house. "Idiot! The guard thought you'd been taken ill, or something. No, I couldn't hear properly but I don't think it was anything like that. Anyway, if it was important we'll hear some time!"

"Don't be smug," said Con crossly. They walked in silence to where the road forked and paused there. "What did you talk to Brychan about?" he asked, in a rather better temper.

"I don't know, lots of things. He's been as far as Londinium, Con, and he was telling me about the journey. Look, I'll come up and see you tomorrow, I should think we can manage one more day away from school. I'm sure your mother will want to cluck over you a little while longer, anyway."

On the other side of the fort the house by the south gate was beginning to settle down after the disturbance of the arrival. Domina Helena had just finished putting her small son to bed and she was combing out Lavinia's long, newly-washed hair when her husband came back from the stockyard, the last of many times.

"There you are, my love," she said to her daughter. "That's nearly dry and the smoky smell has gone. Supper in bed for you tonight."

Lavinia got up unwillingly and looked across at her father, but he was sitting on the bed gazing into some great distance, so there seemed no help for it. She went to kiss him goodnight and he roused himself, putting an arm round her and kissing her forehead where the first soft tendrils of hair were drying.

"Sleep well, sweetheart."

"Are they finally settled?" Domina Helena asked, when the child had gone.

"Yes, I think so. Brychan seems to be good at making himself comfortable. He's fixed up two low trestles from the carpenter's shop to use for beds, and moved in the table. There's water outside, and they should be warm enough."

"I'll go down and take them some supper in a minute. Fabius, there's one thing I don't quite understand. You said that Brychan is going to work for you, and until I saw him that puzzled me rather, because the rest of the time you were talking about him as if he was a new friend. Who is he, exactly?"

"Can't a workman be a friend?" He looked across at her, serious and tired, then his face lightened. "No, Helena, I'm sorry, I do understand what you mean, but I can't answer your question yet. I think there are things about all of us that we don't show at once to strangers, and it seems that there is more than usual still to be found out about Brychan, if he chooses to let us know it."

Lavinia came back into the room in her under-tunic, with a cloak wrapped around her. "Mother, I can't find Crumple. She ran away when everyone came in, and I thought she'd come back, but she hasn't."

"Can't you be without your cat for one night?" asked her mother wearily. "You are meant to be in bed, you know."

"But I didn't have her last night either, that's why it's important."

Fabius smiled at his wife. "I'll look for Crumple in the garden, or Vinny will never sleep!"

"Then I'd better come too," said Lavinia. "She won't come if you call her. Yes, Mother, I did put my sandals on."

She led her father down the path between the apple trees, already flat, dark, shadows with their tight clusters of buds still closed. At the bottom a great oak tree grew in the fence that divided the garden from the muddy path beyond, near the gate that led to the stockyard. Fabius could think of many things he would rather be doing, weary as he was, but the small striped cat that he had bought Lavinia for a birthday present the year before was very dear to her. She had come from the captain of one of the grain-ships that moored at the town quay, and cats were still too rare in Britain to be bought easily. Moreover Crumple, though shy, was a pretty little creature.

"Oh," said Lavinia, stopping abruptly, "but who . . . ?"

Fabius stepped past her, expecting a sailor, prowling in the half-light. The silhouette of a young man, balancing on the top of the fence, showed against the lighter sky beyond. He was steadying himself against the trunk of the tree with one hand while with the other he held something against the breast of his tunic. The architect recognised the short compact shape of Brychan.

"Were you looking for this little creature?" he asked, climbing down on to the woodpile below the fence.

"Crumple! But she hates strangers," said Lavinia.

Brychan disentangled the clinging claws from his tunic and handed the small fluffy animal down into her arms. Crumple buried her nose in Vinny's armpit; then she noticed Fabius, crawled over her mistress's shoulder, jumped down and stalked away into the shelter of the vegetable garden, her dignity spoiled by the fluffy waddle of her hind legs. Once there she sat down, looked over her shoulder disapprovingly and started to wash.

Brychan laughed. "I seem to be honoured, Lavinia. As I came through from the stockyard I heard the little creature crying up there. I think we must have frightened her earlier, but this time she let me take her from the lower branches."

Lavinia went back towards the house ahead of the two men, shooing her cat before her. "Are you warm enough out there?" asked Fabius.

"Yes, indeed. I've made a little fire of shavings and off-cuts, it's comforting to look at in the dark."

Helena met them at the entrance to the atrium with a tray in her hands. "I was just coming down to you, Brychan. There's soup here, will the old man eat that? And bread and meat for you."

Brychan took the tray from her. "Domina Helena, for the first time in a long while I think we are at home, and I thank you." He made a little bow over the steaming bowls, and then turned to Fabius. "In the morning I shall be ready to start work, sir, and it will be a good feeling; it's too long since I was among wood and stone and practical things. Good-night."

Helena went back into the kitchen. Fabius watched her as she took the soup from Antonia's shaky hands and carried it into the little dining room; her skin was very smooth and clear, and in the soft glow of the lamp-light she did not look old enough to be Lavinia's mother. She felt his eyes on her and looked up, smiling.

"What is it?"

"Oh, nothing, only that it's good to be back home. Yester-day reminded me of dangers I hadn't thought about for months, and now, here, I feel again that nothing can touch us." But as he ate his soup in the quiet room in the town that had hushed towards the night, he wondered if he meant it. He too had seen horses ridden hard towards the Praetorium, and heard a little of what the Centurion Aemilius had said to Vericus the night before.

When Helena came back with the rest of their meal he was sitting again looking at something she could not see. "You're very thoughtful tonight. Is it only because you're tired?" she asked.

"Yes, I suppose so. This time it was something Brychan said that started me. When you gave him the food just now, he told you he felt that he had come home. From some people that would only be politeness, but I think he meant it."

5

The Witness of Brychan

Next morning it rained again and Con was miserable. The evening before, his mother, who was inclined to fuss about her only surviving child, had decided that he had a fever, and that he should have come down from the farm in the wagon with Amphibalus. Also his father was not expected home that night, so there would be no chance of finding out from him the answers to some of the questions that were puzzling him. Realising that it would save time in the end Con went to bed, allowed his mother to undo Brychan's excellent bandaging and anoint him with her favourite salve, and drank the hot posset she brought him, with as good a grace as he could manage.

He had hoped that Julius would come for him early the next day, but when he woke to the damp chill of rain, and the gloom of a roof of cloud stretching south from the hills, he knew there was no chance of that. He lay humped in bed until mid-morning, when he decided that whatever his mother said, he would be warmer up and dressed. The shallow burns on his chest were no longer troubling him, and his arm only hurt when he used it. He found, however, that this made it impossible to do most of the interesting things he had got up for, such as rebinding the handle of his hunting knife, and giving more thought to the unreliable thong on the model balista he was making.

When he had sat glaring at it for half an hour he understood to his surprise that what he had considered to be his normal good temper was only the result of being usually healthy enough to do the active things that he enjoyed. This made him laugh, because he realised that Julius must have known this about him for a long time. Then he wondered if the differences he had always accepted between himself and his friend might have anything to do with the autumn four years before when Julius had broken his leg badly. He had been in pain and mostly in bed all that following winter; perhaps he had learned some lessons then and also discovered interests that Con had so far been too blind to notice.

In the early afternoon the clouds lifted, the rain slowed to a drizzle, and then stopped altogether. He was not surprised when Julius arrived soon after. Con's mother was resting after a busy morning in the still-room and his father had not yet come home, so there was no one to stop him going out.

"Where shall we go?" he asked, as soon as they were safely through the gate.

Julius looked up at the sky. "Not far, it'll rain again soon. Let's go and see how Amphibalus is."

Con felt suddenly diffident. "You don't think we shall be in the way? Brychan's supposed to be working."

"He'll tell us if we are. Anyway, there's still Amphibalus. I have a feeling he might be interesting to talk to if he isn't too ill."

On any other day Con might have objected to spending an afternoon visiting a sick old man; if he had been a retired veteran that might have been different, but nothing he knew so far about Amphibalus suggested that he had ever

56

been in the army. Today was different, however, and in spite of everything he had said to his mother the night before, he did not want to walk far.

They skirted the east and south walls of the fort and turned down the alley that led beside Fabius's house to his stock-yard. The wet scaffolding poles piled against the high south wall were steaming in the thin spring sunshine, but the trodden earth between the piles of gravel and rough stone was muddy and full of puddles. The work-room with the store beside it was built against the west side, with two wide doors, both fastened back. Inside a man was singing.

Brychan looked up as they came in, shutting out the afternoon sun. He had pulled a long trestle just inside the door and now he was bending over the piles of tablets and scrolls that had been stored on a rack behind him.

Smiling, he said, "I wondered if the sun would bring you out! Is the arm easier today, Con?"

"Yes, much, though my mother won't stop fussing!"

Julius looked past Brychan to the open store-room door. "Is Amphibalus asleep?"

"I don't think so, I left him looking at some of Caius Fabius's plans. I think he must be a very good architect; it's not easy to be sure just from drawings, but at least you can tell if the proportions are right."

"You wait till you have a chance to talk about proportions to Fabius!" said Con, laughing.

"And then what?" enquired Fabius's amused voice from the doorway behind him.

Con spun round, flushing scarlet. "I was only going to say that Brychan would learn something, only I wasn't going to put it quite so politely," he said. "Honestly, sir, when you talked to us last I was interested."

Julius started to giggle uncontrollably and a mild voice from the store-room enquired, "Have we visitors, Brychan?"

The old man was propped high on his makeshift bed, and they could see at once that the leaden look had faded from his skin, and that his eyes were brighter and more alert. Several rolls of drawings lay across the blanket over his knees.

"Caius Fabius," he said, as the architect came over to him, "this plan for the reconstruction of the amphitheatre at Venta—we passed through there not many days ago and it still seemed in a ruinous state. Was it never put into execution?"

"No, and I was as disappointed over that as over anything I've ever worked on. Some men have no interest in making an old thing useful again. All they want to do is new work, something that will have no other name on but theirs. I know how they feel, but to me there's as much satisfaction, in a different way, in helping to pass something down that might have been lost altogether. After all, towns are like that. Who's ever lived comfortably in a place that's been built all together? It's like a new sandal, not moulded comfortably to what people use it for! Even in Rome, generation after generation has added something, turning clay into wood and wood into stone. You know, I do see what Con meant just now!"

"Go on, sir," said Julius. "We want to hear."

"Well then, Amphibalus mentioned the amphitheatre, and that's an example. Once it was the pride of Venta, one of the finest in Britain. I think none of us here would find any pleasure in seeing wild beasts tearing each other to pieces, but there are plenty of other things to see, military displays, athletics, even religious ceremonies. Britain is a province and the citizens of Rome call us provincials; why? Because we don't even want to be able to live the way they do. And now, when we have little enough to make us raise our eyes beyond the circle of our own damp hills, a City Council lets the one good civic amphitheatre in the west fall into decay and become unsafe. Yet people need somewhere where they can meet together and behave in a civilised way, it's something that has to be practised, all the more so when it doesn't come easily. There are many unemployed craftsmen in these parts who would work for food alone on rebuilding Venta; and what happens? I spent a winter on those plans, and then a month ago I sat fifteen days in Venta trying to talk sense into the Council. Then another section of seating fell in and they lost their nerve."

"I know how you must have felt; just when the need became even more urgent! It's hard to see things break that could be mended, but I think it's worse that they might never be built at all," said Brychan thoughtfully.

Fabius turned back with him into the work-room. "Have you managed to find out what I've got here?" he asked.

"Yes, it's clear enough now, sir. I've got most of the plans sorted out and stowed away. I expect you use some of them over and over again. By tomorrow I shall have made a place for everything."

"Very good, then the first thing after that will be for you to show me where everything is! Perhaps then you'll bring the tallies up to date on what I have in the yard. There were several loads in last month that were never entered, and I don't like running out of things unexpectedly." He turned back to the other room. "Julius, was your father in when you left home?"

"Yes, I think so, he was taking stock pretty much as you are now; the quartermaster had sent down a big requisition for stores. Is everyone expecting that the road to Isca might soon be blocked as well?"

"Oh, I don't think so. The Deisi have come and gone before, you know. It's thirteen years since I came to Caer Taff, when I wasn't much older than Con, and the fort was newly built. We've come a long way since then, and forgotten that the trumpet in the fort can signal more than dinner-time. Sometimes we are made to remember, that's all, and then you find that various tasks which have been overlooked are done in a hurry. I asked where your father was because I want to see him about some stone that was supposed to come by boat from inland."

"I know," said Julius. "The Prefect's marble facing for the new shrine for Mars and the Spirit of the Emperor. I don't think Father has any news of it yet. There must be a delay somewhere, it will be worth its weight in gold when it does come."

"He must think the Spirit of the Emperor is worth it! I think I will walk over and see him though, I've got one or two other things to discuss. Did you know that the Prefect is making a collection towards the new shrine? I think it would be better if all we citizens gave about the same. I suppose in the summer there will be a grand dedication, if all's quiet westward. That will be a great festival, but you'll be gone by then, I suppose, Brychan?"

"Yes, if it's not till summer."

Something about Brychan's voice was strange. Con, perched on the edge of the table, turned to look at him. The young man's face was white; he dropped his head quickly and started to sort through the wax tablets in front of him, but his fingers seemed clumsy.

Into the sudden, small silence Con said quietly, "What is it, Brychan? Would you not have gone to the festival if you had been here?"

Brychan looked up, straight ahead of him, his fingers

THE WITNESS OF BRYCHAN

whitening against the tablet he held. "No, I would not have gone."

Fabius said, "Two nights ago at Vericus's farm you did not pray with us, Brychan; was it for the same reason?"

"Yes."

"I'm sorry, Brychan," said Fabius. "I think we've asked too many questions, or not enough. I was stupid not to have understood before what your secret was. If I had I could have sent the boys away and asked you quietly, just between the two of us. I think it's gone too far for that now. Con, you probably didn't understand where your question was leading, so what Brychan says will surprise you. I think he trusts us enough now to tell us that he is a Christian."

Brychan pushed back his stool and stood up. The room was darker and very quiet now, with no sound but the slight roughness of Amphibalus's breathing in the store.

The young man smiled suddenly, looking at their solemn faces. "Yes, Fabius is right, I am a Christian, and a priest of the Christian Church."

"And my father said only last week . . ." said Julius, and stopped.

"I can guess what your father said." Brychan was serious again. "He came back from the bath-house and said, 'I hear the Emperor's taking a firm line with those Christians at last. Time that sort of thing was stamped out once and for all, all those peasants not paying their taxes and sacrificing babies; no wonder trade's bad'."

"Oh Brychan, how did you know?" gasped Julius.

"Because I heard it in every inn from Londinium to Venta, I suppose. We travelled a few days behind the news of the Emperor's Interdict, Amphibalus and I. By now we are well used to what the people of Britain think about the Christians most of them have never met."

There was a sudden drumming on the roof of the store, and the yard outside was blotted out by a veil of rain.

"Caius Fabius," said Amphibalus from the next room, "we had hoped that in staying here we would not be embarrassing you or bringing you into danger, so long as our beliefs were not known. Perhaps now it would be better if we left before nightfall. I find I am much stronger already."

Fabius went over to the doorway. "Amphibalus, even if it had not just begun to rain again I would have told you that you were talking nonsense. I hope I am a loyal subject of the Emperor, but there are some advantages after all in being a provincial one. We have a little more freedom of thought here in Britain, or at the least, longer to make up our mind to change. I will turn no stranger, least of all a sick one, from under my roof because what he believed in the winter is no longer legal in the spring. I for one do not believe the fabric of the state to be so fragile that it needs that sort of defence. Con, Julius, I know I can trust you both this far, and I believe that Brychan is safe to tell us what he believes, why it's so dangerous, and what brings him to Caer Taff."

Before he spoke, Brychan lit a small pottery lamp that had

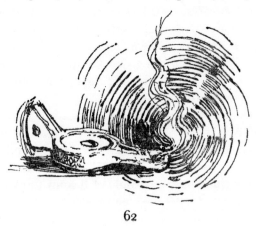

been on the table and carried it through into the store-room. The tenseness had gone from him now, and looking from him to his friend Con saw that neither of them was afraid.

"From the look of that sky not even Vinny will disturb us for an hour at least," Brychan said. "Amphibalus, will it cramp you if I sit on the bed?"

Then, with the boys opposite him, both quiet and more than a little scared by what had happened, and the tall Fabius leaning against the doorpost, he began to speak.

"I am a priest," he said. "In fact we are both priests, and we were travelling back from my ordination to the people I have been sent to serve in the west. I was born near Nidum, as I told you, and although I'm a citizen there is some Silure blood in me, as you must have guessed from my hair. I know the dialects of the west and I was to use them in my work. And now, I suppose, you are wondering how I, who for three days have seemed sane enough, should come to be what the Emperor considers to be an enemy of the state?"

"If you asked Amphibalus, or any other Christian how they were converted part of what they told you would be different, but what was underneath would be the same. It would be easier if I knew you better, but I think I've already come to understand you a little. Fabius, will you tell us, has there ever been a time in your life when the world turned over and lit up from inside, and nothing was ever the same again?"

Fabius was silent for a moment, then he laughed. "Yes, I know what you mean. It was just like that."

"Will you tell us when this happened?"

"Yes of course, if it will help. It was when I knew that Helena loved me, and that we should be able to be married."

"That's rather what I thought you would say. I have met Domina Helena and your daughter, and I know your home is a happy one. So what happened took place because of a person, how you felt for her and how you learned you were loved in return, and that was enough to change everything?"

"Yes."

"That's what it's like for us, when we understand the love of our Master. It isn't only something in our minds, it's a real, practical thing like all true love. It may happen quickly, or only after a long time, but suddenly we know that we are loved in a way that makes it impossible not to love back. That's how it begins, with love, and everything follows from that. Now some of what I'm trying to explain may seem so obvious that you will feel that you've always known that it must be possible, and yet there's a strangeness in its heart that can take you out over the edge of your mind into a country you did not know was there. Because this love I'm talking about isn't quite like any other. It goes beyond the world, and can't be harmed by things that happen in the world. That is what makes it more important to us than the edicts of the state, and why it makes us feel more complete than people whose hearts are set on things that they must leave behind when they die."

"But how can a belief that isn't about this world be dangerous to the state?" asked Julius.

"It isn't quite as simple as that. You see, Christians still have to live with other people, and that's where the difficulties start. Love isn't the simple thing it can seem. It can be demanding, because its standards are different from those usually accepted by the state; and people can be very afraid of anything that seems to ask more than they want to give, even if the demands are not actually being made of them. So sometimes, when this fear is greatest, it is not permitted to be a Christian, and at other times it is."

"It was permitted last year before the Emperor Galienus

died, wasn't it, and then before when we were small and before Diocletian was elected?" asked Con.

"Yes."

"Brychan," said Julius, "when we sacrifice or pray to the Gods of Rome we're usually only showing loyalty to the Emperor, nothing more. Why can't you do it then, if it's such a little thing, and you've said that Christians aren't disloyal to the state?"

"Because if we sacrificed before a statue of Caesar, even though it's something that most men do without believing it means very much, it would show that we accepted Caesar as equally important with our own God, and we don't. We have two obediences, and the one to God must always come first."

Julius looked at him, his face full of distress. "Oh Brychan, why does life have to be like this? There are enough big and terrible things in it without making more. Two days ago we were all nearly killed, and now when that's over what you've told us could put your life in danger again, if someone with my father's ideas knew about it."

"Julius," said Brychan, "don't make the mistake of thinking that ideas aren't dangerous. That's one important thing I've learned from life. What happens in men's minds is every bit as real as what happens in the outside world. In some ways it's more so, because what we think and believe makes us act the way we do. The things in your father's mind and in mine are just as real as the sword that nearly killed you or the soup in Lavinia's pot."

"I suppose I understand that, it's only that I wish it wasn't true. I know it's dark outside because it's raining, but I feel as if a cloud had come over everything else as well!"

"Try not to feel like that, Julius. If anyone needed to it would be me, and I don't. You see, I believe in someone who is both a friend I love and a God I can worship, and if

E 65

Amphibalus and I are in greater danger today than we were two days ago it doesn't change it. If anyone should betray me to the authorities that wouldn't separate me from my Master, it would only send me nearer to him."

"Nobody has said anything about betrayal," said Fabius, who had been silent for some time. "You've started to answer our questions, Brychan, and told us enough, I think, to be certain that it would be wrong for any of us to run out into the rain to denounce you to the Prefect. Now we have to decide what to do until we've had time to understand things better, and one thing is certain: it would be more dangerous for all of us for you to try to leave Caer Taff now, unprepared, than if you stay on quietly as we'd planned until we can see more clearly what you should do."

"Fabius, you have a family to think of, even though no one would suspect these boys of knowing what we are," said Amphibalus in a troubled voice.

"I am thinking of myself when I say that what we must do now, even if it's more difficult than action, is to behave as if nothing has happened. We are well placed between us to find out what's going on in Caer Taff, because although Emperors may make edicts, until the Prefect has sorted out his Deisi raiders he's not going to start hunting for Christians. When he does we shall know."

"I suppose you're right," said Brychan, "though I'm not happy about Con and Julius; I've put them into enough difficulty and confusion already."

"Not unless they do anything foolish now. Listen, both of you. If you should hear anything about the persecution of Christians, don't ask questions and make people think it's something that interests you; and if you do have news come to me with it. From now on this stockyard is out of bounds."

It was still raining as the boys went down the lane to the

main road. There had been nothing more to say, except to promise to obey Fabius and then to take their leave of Brychan; that had not been easy. Now there was the feeling of uncertainty and emptiness, and the closing of a door to somewhere bright but perilous. Now that they would not see Brychan again, life in Caer Taff seemed flat and ordinary. It was too soon, even, to discuss together what they had heard, and they parted quickly at the corner of the fort.

6

High Tide

It was nearly dark by the time Con arrived home, and his
mother was not pleased with him; however, the return of
Aemilius from his mission west towards Nidum gave him a
chance to escape from her anger. He sat down with his
parents to the evening meal neatly dressed in a dry tunic, his
arm newly bandaged, and with nothing more than damp hair
to show that he had been out.

Aemilius was tired and said little during the early part of
the meal; then, when the dishes had been taken away and
he lay back on his couch with a plate of small yellow apples
and the last of the dried figs in front of him, he put down his
wine cup and looked at his son.

"You don't seem much the worse for your experiences!"

"No, Father. I wish though that I'd been down in the
kitchen yard with Julius. Up on the roof I couldn't see what
was going on."

"Perhaps not, but you seem to have been fairly effective."

"Yes, Julius told me. Father, do you remember the first
time you killed anyone?"

"Hush!" said Domina Nigella his mother, a large woman,
sitting decorously in a chair beside her husband's couch.
"That isn't a fit subject for the dining room."

"Perhaps not, my dear," said her husband. "But there are

68

a number of things I want to talk to Con about, connected with the raid."

Domina Nigella gathered her robe around her and stood up. "In that case I shall go to bed. I know that I married a soldier but there are still some things which I prefer not to hear discussed."

Con sat down again after his mother had sailed out of the room, and grinned at his father. "Oh dear!"

"Mm, yes, but you weren't too tactful, Con. Actually I'm glad your mother has gone; you know that we took two prisoners that night?"

"Yes, did we get much out of them?"

"Not a lot, one was pretty far gone when we found him. I hope little Lavinia will never find out quite how effective her boiling soup was. The other man was wounded too, but from what he would tell us, our raid was only one of several along the coast, all timed for the same night. I'd have given a lot to know which chieftain was behind them, but the prisoner didn't tell us that and it's too late now. War can be a filthy business, Con, it's as well you should understand it. I was glad that I was riding west when the interrogations were going on."

"What did you find out? Were the other raids more successful?"

"Only at Moridunum, and things were a shambles there. Otherwise the Deisi were beaten off remarkably effectively, I don't think they'll come again this summer. Moridunum was pretty bad; they got in among the outlying houses, and some of what they did there is not for your ears, let alone your mother's. When I think of you boys and Fabius's child in such danger it makes me want to keep you locked up all summer, except that I know it wouldn't work."

Con laughed, though he had a considerable respect for his

69

father's methods of enforcing discipline. "Where are you off to next?" he asked.

"Must I always be away from home?" enquired Aemilius, reaching for a fig.

"Of course not, but you do seem to be away a lot, don't you?"

"I suppose I do, but you can't remember much about the time I was on the scout boats, when you were small. Sometimes we were away for a month at a time then. No, Con, I shall be in Isca for part of the summer, but until then I think the Prefect will use me nearer home."

Con wondered as he went to bed that night if there was any chance that his father might be put to chasing Christians, but it did not seem very likely. He was too good an officer to be wasted on minor police duties.

During the next days Con and Julius saw nothing of Fabius and heard no more of the Emperor's Edict. During the hours of freedom after school before dark there were many things to do as the evenings grew longer. Con was beginning to forget what the priest had told them, but Julius, though he did not talk about it, was often quieter and more preoccupied than usual.

At the start of the next month a spell of fine weather came in time for another school holiday. All seemed quiet near Caer Taff and the boys got permission to spend the day on the beach at the mouth of the river, were it joined the estuary by the deep-water moorings.

Con called for Julius early on a morning when for the first time the wind was warm with the promise of summer, and the little town seemed stuffy and hot. Septimius the merchant lived on the road that ran south through the small market below the fort. His warehouse backed on to the river wharfs with the house in front, separated by a courtyard. Julius's mother had been dead for some years, and although Septimius was fond of his son there was none of the warmth in his home that one felt in the houses of Fabius and Aemilius.

Julius was waiting in the open doorway, comfortable in his oldest tunic, his hair very red in the morning sun.

"Father has his head deep in his records," he said, "I told him where we were going and he looked up for long enough to tell me to keep an eye open for his stone barges. The Prefect's marble facing still hasn't come!"

In half an hour they were scrambling down the low cliff above the shore. It was the day of the spring tide and the water was far out, a silver streak almost on the horizon, leaving pale levels of shining mud, cut by the network of water channels that spread out in a complicated delta across the river's three mouths. Dumnonia hung like a dark cloud across the estuary, near the shore patches of sand and shingle lay between the low rocks, barnacle-covered and delightful. Mostly the mud was smooth except for the twisted wormcasts and the boys kept close under the cliff. A long way out a fisherman was catching shrimps, but he knew the ways of the mud, where it was safe, and how the strong tide would run.

They found two rocky pools and spent a contented morning excavating a canal between them.

"Ouff, we haven't done that for ages, I suppose we're getting too old!" said Julius when they stopped at last, muddy and happy, to look at their handiwork. "Have we got anything to eat?"

"Only because I remembered to bring something." Con fished around for the bundle he had left in a dry place with their sandals. "I didn't think we should be back before we were hungry. Look, I thought Father had eaten them all, but I've got the last of the apples."

71

"Oh good, I know those little yellow ones, they're much better than they look. We finished ours weeks ago."

They spread out the end of a loaf of bread, a pat of cream cheese in an oozing cloth and the four wizened apples, and ate in silence, their backs against the last dry sand-dune. The wind was strong so near the water, though low among coarse grass it was warm enough to lie and look at the enormous sky and the trailing mare's-tail clouds. When they sat up again the estuary looked different. The tide was coming in fast and ahead of them the little runnels were filling up and meeting. Already the pools where they had spent the morning had changed and joined into an unfamiliar shape. Far out a cluster of fishing boats and a larger barge were waiting for high water to come in across the shoals of the harbour mouth.

"Look," said Con, pointing, "I wonder if that's your father's marble."

They put on their sandals and walked farther along the shore above the line of the wet sand. Up from the beach, woods swept away to the ridge west of the town, and Vericus's farm. Much of the land near the river was marshy, but there were a few fishermen's huts among the trees, though several of them had been deserted since the time of the raid.

As they turned towards the path that led up the low cliff a man came out of the trees farther ahead and dropped down on to the beach.

Con caught Julius's arm. "Look, quick, isn't that Brychan?"

"Surely it can't be." Julius shaded his eyes against the bright afternoon sunlight. "What could he be doing out here?"

"Let's find out."

Closer to, Brychan's bright hair was unmistakable. He heard them coming as they slipped on the shingle and turned

73

quickly. There had been a loneliness about him as he stood watching the wave ridges rushing in, but it was gone in his greeting.

"It's good to see you again!"

Julius's serious face lit up with pleasure. "I was sure that you would have gone west already, only Fabius had decided not to tell us. It's been so quiet."

"Not quite quiet enough," said Brychan. "Fabius believes that the Prefect will make a move soon now. An officer from the staff of the Legate himself came yesterday. It wasn't officially announced why, though the Praetorium tried to give the impression that it was to receive a report about the Deisi raiding. Fabius's confidant at the officers' bath-house seemed to think there was more to it than that, and I don't see what else it can be but the Edict."

"Then if things are becoming dangerous again, what are you doing out here?" asked Con.

"Not just watching the tide come in! It's like this. Amphibalus is very much better, but I still don't think he could stand the journey to Nidum by road; besides, there are armed checkpoints that way. The guards are questioning everyone who leaves by the west gate. I think the only way out of Caer Taff now is by sea. If I can get Amphibalus safely as far as one of the huts up there in the woods I don't think it will take long to find a fishing boat going the right way. And the fishermen hereabout are independent men, they don't ask questions if no one troubles them."

"Have you found what you were looking for?" asked Julius.

"Yes, near enough. Fabius thought it would be safer if I came myself. No one knows me down here, though someone might wonder what he was doing poking about alone. But I don't think I'd better tell you any more."

"No," said Con, "I suppose not, but is there anything we can do to help when the time comes?"

"Not if all my plans go right. No, Julius, don't look like that, you do understand, don't you? Who knows, next year the Edict may be changed and one day I shall ride in from the west and we can all sit round Fabius's table and talk till morning. But until then, how can I put two boys of your age who are not Christians into what might be great danger?"

"Would it be different if we were Christians?" asked Julius.

"Yes . . . though I should still not take your help willingly. You see, you don't even know why you want to, do you, except that it's a personal thing? And when you stop to think about it, why should one man you've only known a few days turn you from all that your fathers have bred into you in sixteen years? It doesn't make sense."

"No, it doesn't," said Con. "Except that though we may not understand what we're doing, we are trying to do what's right, and we can't help it if we like you!"

Brychan stood looking at them, with the freshening wind pulling at his short brown cloak. There was a strength and quietness in his face that they had never seen in anyone before, something that showed in his deep-set eyes, and a mouth that was wide and firm without being heavy.

It seemed for the moment that there was nothing more that he could say, and he turned back towards the water. The tide was almost up, advancing the last yards over the beach in a pattern of fan-shaped ripples; the air was loud with the hiss of foam and the muffled roar of the undertow across the pebbles. The boys turned and watched it with him. It was as if this was the first high tide they had seen. There was something beautiful and inexorable about it that they had never felt before.

Brychan bent for a flat stone and sent it scudding and jumping across the wave crests.

"Can you do that? Julius won't believe it's easy!" Con's stone hopped one jump less than Brychan's. They threw again, laughing, the tension broken, as the waves lapped unnoticed almost to their feet. Julius threw a piece of water-smoothed driftwood but the next wave carried it back and splashed his sandals.

They climbed back on to a sand-dune as the water began to scour along the crackling seaweed of the high-tide line, sucking it back to float or sink among the patterns of scum on the inshore water.

"That's why I like high tide," said Brychan, pointing. "It's clean and strong, it clears away all the rubbish the ebb tide leaves on the shore."

"Look how high the water's coming. Right past the usual tide mark." Con climbed farther back.

"This is the spring tide. I can understand how my ancestors must have found something magical about it. It has so much power, though here the water doesn't roar up in a great wall as it does where the estuary narrows. But when I watch the tide it makes a picture in my mind of something else; I think how for three hundred years men like me have travelled and preached. Sometimes the little lights they have tried to kindle have gone out, but there were always more, many more, to follow them. The message they carried was like a tide; each single wave falls back, but the other waves pass it, and the time will come when the spring tide will run, higher and stronger than ever before, and all the little waves will have been part of it."

"Brychan, do you think that could possibly happen soon?" asked Julius.

"I don't know. It isn't important that we should know the

times of things, only that we should believe in them and hope for them."

Con looked at the two of them, not fully understanding, feeling that Julius was going away ahead of him to somewhere he was afraid of. For a moment he was glad that perhaps Brychan would soon be far away and they might never see him again. Certainly a part of his life had been more comfortable and certain before this strange young man had come into it, but comfort at least was not one of the things that he had expected from life, and he was beginning to wonder too about the value of certainty. Brychan had opened his mind to things that had happened beyond his own hills, and to ways of thought that he had not known existed, and something in himself had answered the new voice. Perhaps this shaking free of the mind was easier for Julius, but if there was indeed a journey to be made in a manner beyond his imagination, then Julius would not take it alone.

7

The Sacrifice of Albanus

School started very early, so Con was surprised the morning after the high tide to find Julius waiting for him a little way down the road, not long after dawn.

"Whatever is it? Couldn't it wait until break?" he asked, yawning.

"No. Listen, Con, this is serious. My father told me last night that there's a rumour that Christians are hiding somewhere in the town. He says the Prefect knows about it, and he's going to do something soon. The watch on the roads is still supposed to be because of the Deisi, but it isn't."

Con stopped in his tracks. "Then we must tell Fabius at once. I don't know when Brychan was planning to get away, but it'll have to be immediately now."

"But how can we get a message to Fabius? If we miss school there'll be trouble, and questions asked that we can't answer."

"Wait a minute, I suppose we could go to Fabius's house in the noon break, but it might be too late for him to arrange anything today." He looked down at his arm, which was still lightly bandaged. "There's nothing else for it, I shall have to have a relapse. Tell the master my arm looked angry and I've gone to let the surgeon look at it, if he should miss me. I'll be as quick as I can."

They had reached the corner of the fort and there were few people about so early; Con ran across the road and down the alley that lay beside the house of Fabius. Mindful that he was not to go into the stockyard, he went in at the garden gate and up through the orchard to the back of the house.

Fabius was finishing his breakfast, sitting on the terrace beyond the atrium, in the first warmth of a fine morning. When he saw Con he let the scroll in his hand roll up on itself and came down the path to meet him.

"Con, what is it?"

The boy stopped behind an apple tree heavy with blossom that hid him from the house. He was breathless, and suddenly a little frightened, for Fabius was looking at him gravely.

"Julius's father told him that there were Christians hiding in Caer Taff, sir. We thought you should know at once."

"But you'll be missed from school!" Con held up his arm. "Oh, I see, that was a good idea. You were right to come—if the rumour is strong enough to have reached Septimius then the danger is very close."

He turned away, clasping and unclasping his hands; the small scroll he was still holding crackled and he looked down in surprise before thrusting it into the breast of his long tunic.

"I mustn't leave that lying about, it belongs to Brychan. Well, there's nothing else for it, they must go today, though I don't see how. It's easy enough to think of an excuse to send a wagon out of the town, but I don't know who could drive it; I was planning to do it myself, but I have an appointment to see the Prefect this afternoon, and they must be clear of the town in daylight or the guards won't let them through."

Con said, "Sir, couldn't we . . . ?"

79

Fabius looked at him, then he said, "Come up to the house, I must think."

Con's mind was working fast as he followed the architect into the atrium. It would be just possible after school finished midway through the afternoon. They must drive one of Septimius's wagons to the back gate of the stockyard. It would have to be Septimius's wagon to provide a reason for Julius to drive it, but Fabius had often borrowed one before, and no one would look very hard at two boys driving alone. If Fabius was actually at the Praetorium so much the better, it was a perfect cover.

Domina Helena was standing at the window of Lavinia's room above the main door; the child had been sick in the night and was still in bed, cheerful now but very pale. From the window she looked down through the light well to the atrium and saw her husband sitting on the raised edge of the pool.

"That's strange, there's Con down there talking to your father. I wonder what he's doing here at this time of day. They look serious, I hope no one's ill."

"I didn't think anyone could be as ill as I was last night. I was sick four times!"

"I remember, darling, I was there, we had a busy night! Vinny, cover yourself up properly or you'll get a fever!"

"I can't, Crumple's lying on most of the blanket. I've only got this little bit at the top."

Domina Helena picked the cat off the end of the bed and put her on the floor. Crumple shook herself crossly and skipped out of the open window.

"Does she often do that?" asked Domina Helena anxiously.

"Oh yes, she goes round the hole in the middle and over the dining room to the kitchen roof. It's low enough to get down to the garden from there."

THE SACRIFICE OF ALBANUS

"I like this room with its windows facing both ways," said her mother. "Oh, Con seems to have finished. I wonder what they were talking about. He looks pleased and your father doesn't. Now, are you all right for the moment? I must go back to the garden and you should be asleep. There'll be no getting under Brychan's feet in the stockyard today." She closed the door firmly before Lavinia had time to do more than open her mouth.

* * * *

The day followed the pattern of so many along the coast and clouded over after a fine morning; by mid-afternoon it was spitting with rain, the wind blew chill off the estuary, and the two guards on the south road had found themselves a sheltered but smelly corner under the wall of a byre. Men were beginning to come in from the fields, and there were a few small carts bringing up the morning catch from the fishers by the river mouth. No one had come south for some time except a couple of market women who had packed up early, so the guards heard the wheels of a heavy wagon long before it stopped beside them, with the oxen snorting and steaming.

The two boys up on the driver's seat had sacks over their shoulders to keep off the rain.

"Going down to get a load of stone for the Prefect. That's all right, isn't it?" called down the one with red hair.

"A bit late, aren't you?" said one of the men, going round to the back; but the wagon seemed to be empty except for a pile of straw for packing and a folded canvas cover.

"Yes, my father's man went sick, but we can't keep the Prefect waiting. We might not get back till morning."

"Good luck to you, it'll be down heavyish any time now."

He slapped the nearside ox and went back to his friend and the dry length of wall.

The two boys said nothing to each other as the cart lurched away and out of sight down the road to the shore. Then Con said, "There's some way yet. Julius, how are you going to explain to your father?"

"I don't know now, it depends what he finds out. I've fixed things with the yard man, so with any luck it will be only me he misses. But whatever happens we must get back tonight. You can talk us past the guard next time, it'll probably still be raining, and they should have changed, which will be a help."

"I don't know if being a centurion's son will be any use, but I can try." Con looked behind him into the wagon. It must be miserably uncomfortable jolting under that wet straw. He hoped that Amphibalus could stand it.

Then the rain began in earnest. The trees grew thinly here and there was nowhere to shelter, so they drove on, pressed together for warmth, hardly able to see as far as the oxen's horns. The road became a muddy river, with grass and small twigs swept down the deep ruts on either side, it was difficult to avoid the potholes. The cart lurched along for a while and then developed a wobble on the nearside. Julius pulled on the reins to stop but it was already too late, there was a last wrenching as a back wheel jerked and spun above a hole and then the shock as it met the road again forced out the loosened pin, the axle squealed and the cart swayed over at an angle.

Julius leapt down and ran to the beasts' heads as they lowed in protest, while Con, who had nearly been thrown out of his seat, went to the back. The canvas cover was heaving and a leg stuck through the straw. Con burrowed in it till Brychan managed to crawl out, crimson-faced and with straw in his hair.

"Are you all right?" asked Con.

Brychan grinned. "I suppose I don't look it! No more do you, are you swimming out there?"

"It was the wheel."

"I know, that last bump nearly broke my back. Let me have a look." He climbed down as Amphibalus's face appeared from under the wet canvas.

"Shall I get out?" he asked. "Would it be easier?"

Brychan straightened up to say, "No, you're better there, if you can keep dry. I don't think your weight should make much difference." Then he ducked back into the ditch beside the road.

Julius came up. "I've hobbled those two. Is the damage bad?"

Brychan rolled the wheel back on to the road and squatted down to examine it. "This looks sound enough, I think it was only the pin. You should tell your father to make sure his man keeps the wagons properly maintained. I wasn't bred on a farm for nothing. Now we need something to replace it."

He threw off the cloak that was flapping round him like wet seaweed and drew a knife from his belt. By the time Con had cleared out the splintered remains of the old pin he was back, trimming the short thick branch from an elder tree.

"This should hold for long enough; now will you two stand ready with the wheel while I lift the wagon?"

"You can't do it alone," objected Julius.

"Why not? I'm no taller than you but I've got broader shoulders. Hurry now, it'll be dark early tonight, and I want to get out of the rain."

He turned his back on the wagon, got a good grip on the sloping axle and heaved. The rain ran down his face and neck in rivulets and his sandals slipped in the mud.

"Once more," he said, grinning through the wet.

The wagon tilted slowly, Con caught the end of the axle and Julius fitted on the wheel. Brychan called, "Lie still while I get the peg in, Amphibalus." He hammered it home, wedged it with smaller splinters and then straightened up, wiping his hands on the seat of his soaking tunic.

"I hope there's some dry wood in your hut, Brychan," said Con. "I've never seen anyone who needed a wash as much as you do!"

"As all three of us! Julius, I'll drive now, it should be safe enough and I know the way from here."

Above the last slope that led down to the lower wharf he turned off along a side track that disappeared under the trees. The wagon slid and squelched across the mud until they were out of sight of the road, then he drove in under the end of a row of fir trees and stopped.

"We'll have to leave the cart and walk from here. At least there's grass for the poor beasts."

They went round to the back of the wagon; there were

84

blankets and two small sacks of food under the straw beside Amphibalus, and the satchel Brychan had been carrying when they first met him. The old man crawled out from under the canvas and sat on the end of the floor.

Brychan looked at him thoughtfully. "I think I must carry you, Father, it's not far now. Will you get up on to my back? It's not dignified, but you'll be more comfortable."

They were a strange procession, with Brychan ahead, and the boys carrying provisions and wet blankets. Somehow the rain that had soaked and chilled them had washed away the fear that had been knotting Julius's stomach all day, and even the thought of what they must explain to their parents when they returned home later that night seemed less important. The need for a roof and a fire was more urgent than the memory of danger.

The hut Brychan had found was well hidden, built into a bank behind a screen of hollies, and it had not long been abandoned. The door had gone, but Con fixed the canvas cover on to the pegs that had held it; there was a blackened hearth against one of the walls, under the smoke hole, and a pile of dry straw in a corner.

Amphibalus sniffed at it. "This has had a winter's use already, but we can get clean branches tomorrow. I've slept on much worse."

Brychan came in with an armful of short sticks, dragging a rotten branch. "There's some dry wood at the bottom of the pile, we must put the big stuff round when we get a fire going."

Con stacked the stores at the back of the hut and then went to help Brychan with the fire. Julius stood watching them, feeling suddenly overwhelmingly tired, shivering in his wet clothes. Then the first bright flames licked up among the twigs and shadows danced over the rough daubed walls.

Amphibalus began to divide the pile of bedding and Julius went to help him.

The fire caught quickly and they squatted round it holding out the steaming blankets. The hut smelt of wet wool and the moss that grew on the logs as they spat and dried around the fire.

"This is like your aunt's cottage, Brychan," said Amphibalus. "Do you remember?"

"The first night? How could I forget that!"

Con looked at them; they seemed to be sharing some old memory. Brychan saw his gaze.

"It was seven years ago, the day I first met Amphibalus; we were along the coast from here at Nidum, but that's a long story."

"Too long to tell us now? And if not now when, I wonder," said Julius. There was a crash of thunder overhead. "We can't go home till the worst of the storm's over and that won't be for a while yet. Tell us, Brychan, there haven't been many times when you could talk to us about yourself."

"This is Amphibalus's story, really." He turned to the old man. "Are you too tired tonight, Father?"

"Not for this story, ever."

"Wait a minute," said Con. "Why is Brychan calling you Father all of a sudden?"

"Ah, I think the story will tell you that, but you will have noticed that he only does it when we are with friends. Now, all this began seven years ago, as Brychan said. That summer I was far east of here at Verulamium. I think you would be too young to remember how things were then for us Christians. We had been persecuted before but never as we were then. The edict of the Emperor in the east had spread across the provinces and touched us like a creeping plague. But

86

persecution is a strange thing, for in one way it makes life very simple."

"How do you mean, simple?" asked Con.

"Think how complicated life is for most of us after we've grown up. It's an endless round of decisions. If we're lucky they aren't just 'Where can I find food today?', but 'Can I afford that slave I need? How shall I educate my son?', things like that. Persecution changes all this, you no longer plan for a future that may now never happen, and it leaves you free with only one question left. 'Is what I believe so true that I will die for it?' Once you are past that there is only the waiting."

"I don't understand how anyone can believe in a thing enough to die for it," said Julius. "Not the way your people have to die. It must be terrible, being arrested and questioned, as if the State was a wall you had been sheltering under and it suddenly fell and crushed you."

"Don't you see, Julius, that's the trouble. We accept all that our rulers do as long as it makes life easier for us, but there are times when we must put our backs to your wall and say, 'Enough, no further.' When the Deisi attacked the farm where you were sheltering you wouldn't have sat down and not helped to defend your friends, would you? And if they'd got hold of you and tried to make you tell where the women were hiding you wouldn't have answered easily?"

Julius remembered little Lavinia darting through the smoke with her pot of soup. "No, I wouldn't, or I would have tried not to. After the kitchen gate fell in I thought, 'Let me die, and get it over quickly, and then let the others be safe.' It was like a prayer really, only I don't know who I thought would hear."

"You see," said Amphibalus with a smile, "you do know how one can be prepared to die for a person or a belief, and

87

when you are a Christian it's the same thing. That summer someone died for me."

"In Verulamium?" asked Con.

"Yes, his name was Albanus, and from one point of view I hardly knew him. I said just now that when persecution comes there is nothing to do but wait. I didn't mean that one must go out and look for death, though I know some of the brethren have done just that. I believe that is wasting the life we have been given, and when one is a priest the choice may not be in one's own hands. We have been chosen by the church to be the shepherds of our people, and usually a live shepherd is better than a dead one. The people with whom I lived had begged me to go, but I was waiting for a message from my bishop. The guard were already beating on the front door of my house as I left by the back gate. The city gates were closed for the night as I ran in the darkness, not thinking where I was going, but my feet were guided, for a friendly door opened and I was pulled inside."

"By Albanus? Wasn't he a Christian?"

"No, but he had heard the hue and cry, and he told me quite simply that he did not like to see anything chased. I think he would have handed me over to the guards if he had found out I was a murderer, but as it was I stayed in his house for seven days. That was the time it took for him to come under suspicion. The authorities knew I must still be in the town, and they thought that someone would inform on me."

"And they did?" asked Julius.

"I suppose so, but I never knew who did it. Not one of Albanus's household anyway, he was well served. He was quartermaster to the garrison and I think it never occurred to his men to question who their master's guest was. We talked together during those days as I have seldom talked

88

with any man, almost without a pause. Ours is a faith that is most often passed from one to another by example, not by words, but this was a time when it was mind to mind. Albanus had a good brain, but he was a simple man. I answered questions that he had been asking long before we met; once his mind was satisfied he took the next step forward as if it was the most obvious thing in the world."

"You mean he became a Christian, just like that, in a few days?" Con looked as if he did not believe it.

"It need not take very long, you know." Amphibalus laughed. "Usually we would make a convert wait for his actual baptism till he is very sure, but this time I baptised Albanus in his own bathroom, and the next day the guards came to search his house. I was asleep, for it was very early in the morning, but I woke to see him bending over me in the half-light to take my cloak. It was a big one, dark, with a large hood, good for travelling but too distinctive for a man on the run. I did not understand until he turned in the doorway and said, 'Goodbye' with a strange look in his eyes. I knew then, but before I could reach him he had shut the door and fastened it on the outside. It was then that I heard the guard beating on the main gate below. Much later one of the servants let me out and gave me the money and clothes that Albanus had prepared for me. I did not hear the full story of what had happened for some time, and then it was in an inn at Venta, told by one soldier to another."

"It was a good death, Amphibalus, and you know that now," said Brychan from his place across the fire. "Though it wasn't clear to you yet when we first met."

"Yes, please, you still haven't told us that," said Julius.

"Have I not, and this story should be as much about Brychan as about me! Well, after that evening in Venta I went out and walked where my feet took me, for it was night in my mind as well. I knew that Albanus, dressed in my cloak, had been taken for me in the half-light, but not till then that he was dead, beheaded after many days of questioning. But before the next dawn I began to see that my Lord must have some work prepared for me, and I thought I could see what it was. Perhaps I had been saved twice over because I was a priest. I thought of how over the generations something most precious had been given carefully from one pair of hands to another, not because it was fragile but because it was such a costly gift. I prayed that I in my turn should be shown someone to whom I could hand on this gift; I did not ask for a sign, but when one came I knew it. I was on the shore below Nidum. I had been set down there by a fishing boat, not too near the fort up river. It was almost dark and I was looking for a night's lodging when a boy with red hair came up to me.

" 'Are you lost?' he asked. 'It's a cold night to be far from home. Will you come in and warm yourself by our fire?' "

Con looked at Brychan. "Why did you do that?" he asked. "Were you a Christian then?"

"Why? I didn't know at the time, and no, I was far from being a Christian, I'd scarcely heard of them. I was a boy of your own age come to help his aunt at harvest time."

"It was my harvest," said Amphibalus quietly.

Brychan had looked away again and was gazing into the fire. "And do you not call the man who gave you life your father?" he said.

It was quiet then in the hut, except for the drip of rain from the roof, and Con understood that something new had happened between them all, as they sat so close together. He thought that Brychan must be praying now, although it was not like any prayer that he had seen before. Then he began to be uneasy; perhaps this God of Brychan had brought him here with Julius tonight just as it had happened seven years before that Brychan had met Amphibalus. That was too strange and terrible to think about. He wanted to be safe back on the road to Caer Taff with everything over and no more Brychan to make life difficult and dangerous, and to put things in Julius's head that he did not understand.

He got up and went to the curtain over the door. It was dusk outside but the rain was easing off. The draught of cold air made the others stir and shiver.

"You must be on your way," said Brychan, coming over to him, "and may you reach home safely. You've already taken risks we would never have allowed if there had been any other way and Amphibalus had been stronger."

Julius got up unwillingly. "But we came, and whatever else happens tonight I'm glad we did. Brychan, bless us before we go. You can do it, can't you, even though we aren't Christians?"

"Yes," said Brychan. "I can do it."

8

An Affair for the State

By the time the wagon was safely put away in the yard beside Septimius's warehouse Con was so tired that he could hardly think. It was very late and it had taken all his persuasion, and the good luck that one of the guards was from his father's old century and knew him, to get them back into the town at all. And now, more clearly than ever, he realised that the difficult part was still ahead. He had never been out as late as this before when his father did not know where he was; it was not a habit that was encouraged in a frontier town.

The boys walked back together to the gate at the front of the merchant's house and then stopped. Con could see that Julius was quite as weary as he was himself, his limp had come back as it sometimes did, also his father Septimius was notoriously quick-tempered. His own father had been trained over the years to keep his emotions in check. Septimius had not, and for all his business sense was inclined to strike first and think afterwards. Also there was the matter of the wagon. Julius had a story ready to explain that, but it would be better if he did not have to use it.

"Good luck!" he said. "I'll see you in the morning, I hope." He ran on up the road towards the fort.

As he reached the market place the moon came out from

the clouds and the last of the drizzle stopped. He stumbled across the deserted space, with its litter of damaged vegetables and the lingering smell of fish, and turned the eastern corner of the fort. A lantern flashed ahead across the puddles, and a voice called to him.

A man came out of the dark wrapped from the wildness of the night in an old army cloak, the flaring lantern held high.

"All right, Aulus, it's me," Con called. "I'm here, we were caught in the rain."

It was his father's batman. Con hoped that the whole cohort was not out looking for him. "It's two hours before midnight and your father's not pleased," said the man.

"I'm sorry I got you out on so wild a night," said Con, but the man did not answer as he turned and lit the way across the cart ruts for the short distance along the eastern side of the fort to where they could see the lights of the house. They were streaming out through the open door past the black shape of a man.

"Father," called Con, quickening his pace.

Aemilius turned towards him. "Con? Where have you been all this time? Your mother's in tears with worry and I was just going to turn out the guard."

"I'm sorry, we didn't think it was going to rain for so long, so we sheltered, and then the storm seemed to last for ever."

"Sorry! Wait, perhaps you'd better put a dry tunic on and show your mother you're alive, then come back to me here."

The man Aulus gave him a strange look as Con dropped his sodden cloak on to a bench and went to his mother's room. The next few minutes gave him some idea what to expect from his father. When he came back into the atrium, dry and a little cleaner, Aemilius was warming his hands over a brazier, for the rain had made the night as cold as autumn.

"Come into the dining room," he said, his face unsmiling. "It's warm there and I want to talk to you."

Con followed his father. A lamp still burned on its stand. Aemilius poured himself some wine, and sat down on the edge of the middle couch behind the small table. It gave him the look of an officer receiving a report.

"Sit down, Con," he said. "I don't want to be cross with you for no reason, but perhaps you are beginning to realise the amount of disturbance you have already caused, and I'm curious to know what you considered worth upsetting the whole household for."

Con looked down at the floor, he had expected some kind of questioning, but not this formality. He had never lied to his father before, and a part of himself rebelled even now against the need for it, but this secret was not his to tell.

"There was a bitch, Father. One of the boys told Julius that her puppies were particularly good, and his father was looking for another guard dog. One of the fishermen had her down by the lower harbour and we thought there would be time to go after school."

"Were the puppies so outstanding? Did Julius choose one?"

"No, it turned out they were all bitches."

"How many were there in the litter?"

"Two, no it was three."

"And all bitches, you surprise me! Con, will you stop telling lies and explain where you really went?"

Con glanced up quickly, his face flaming. His father was looking at him with an expression he had never seen before, the fingers of his right hand closing and unclosing about the stem of the wine cup. He dropped his head again and said nothing.

"I think I can begin the story for you," said Aemilius. "This evening at the bath-house the master of the garrison school spoke to me. He was sorry that your arm was troubling you again, and hoped that the surgeon's report on it had been favourable. I don't think that he guessed I was hearing the news for the first time, but I was not pleased to deduce from his enquiry that you had played truant from school this morning, and I came home early to ask you about it. At the moment the only explanation I can think of, and it doesn't seem a likely one, is that you have found yourself a girl from one of the fisher families."

"No!"

"I said I didn't think it was likely. Now, Constantine, will you answer my question?"

Con got up quickly and stood holding on to the edge of the table. "Father, I can't. I didn't want to tell lies to you to start with, only it seemed the best thing to do. Now I'm not going to invent any more, and I can't tell you the truth because it isn't my secret. I'm sorry, but I can't."

He felt that he was shivering and hoped that his father would not notice; then he looked Aemilius in the face, and was more frightened than he had ever been in his life before.

His father stood up. "Does this secret concern Julius?"

"Only partly."

"Very well. My own father would have beaten the truth out of me, but I'm not prepared to do that to you when a night's sleep may make you think more sensibly. However, punishing you tomorrow may be another matter. Go to your room and stay there. I'm not going to lock you in. I don't think you will run away, and there's no need to cause gossip among the servants. I will see you in the morning."

Aemilius strode past Con into the shadows outside. The boy waited a moment, till he heard a door shut across the atrium and then ran to his own room through the darkened house. It was cold; he sat down on the bed and pulled a blanket round his shoulders, too weary to undress. His mind was churning over and over as if he had a fever; he could think of nothing that he could say to his father in the morning, or of any way that what had happened could have been done differently. Only one thing seemed important, that it would be wrong for Brychan to suffer for no other reason than that he was a Christian. Everything else had happened because of that, the disobedience and the lies, and the pain that might yet come.

Con felt his thoughts grow quieter as his body began to relax. He kicked off his sandals, and curled up on the bed fully dressed, still shivering under the blanket.

He woke before dawn with the sickening lurch that comes when sleep has blotted out some great problem only for the morning to bring it back as bad as ever. Now that his body was no longer exhausted he knew there would be no more sleep for him; he lay for a long while watching the grey light grow in the little room, and listening to the small familiar noises of the household waking up. No one came to call him for school. He wondered what his father had told them. When it was light enough to see he got up and washed himself unusually carefully. Mud from the flooded road seemed ingrained in his feet and legs and under his nails; it took a long time to get properly clean. He dressed and made his bed with military precision; the first sunlight was painting a bright shape on the wall that crept slowly down to the shelf where he kept his model balista. He carried it over to the bed and began to rewind the thongs.

The sound of his father's voice outside in the atrium jolted him out of a weary half-dream, but steps passed the door, and although he could hear people talking he could not be sure who they were. Con began to think about Julius and to wonder if he was at school. If only Septimius had not missed the wagon then his friend was likely to escape with no more than a beating.

Another hour passed and he began to grow hungry. There was still water left in the jug, but he had eaten nothing since the early evening of the day before, and then it had not been much. They had not wanted to take more than they could help of Brychan's stores, which would be difficult to replace. He thought later on that he heard his father go out, but it was not easy to be sure, and the small window of his room looked over the garden.

The morning wore on and the room became warmer. Con put the balista away and lay down again on the bed; he was not hungry now, only sick with fright, and he did not know what he would say when his father spoke to him again.

He woke, confused, from an uncomfortable doze, as the door opened. While Aemilius shut it behind him Con got up quickly and straightened his tunic. He was waiting, very white, with his back against the wall under the window, when his father turned towards him.

Aemilius went over to the bed with its rumpled blanket and sat down, then he looked thoughtfully at his son.

"Con, I've just come from Fabius. He sent me a message early this morning. I was surprised that he did not come himself until I heard what he had to tell me; then I understood why it was safer that he should not be seen to seek me out. Fabius had guessed that I might be in some confusion of thought this morning, and when he saw that he had been right he told me where you had been yesterday evening and why."

G   97

Con turned half away from his father until he could stop his lips trembling. He felt as if all the breath had been knocked out of his body.

"Come and sit down," said Aemilius. "There's no need now for me to ask you the same questions as last night, but I've got to have a talk with you."

Con sat down, still not looking at his father. The fear had gone but the confusion remained. Aemilius began to talk quietly as if it was difficult.

"I suppose I could have guessed last night what had happened, except that I was too angry. I realised on the night of the raid that Brychan and his friend were Christians." Con drew in his breath to speak but his father hushed him. "No, wait, let me finish, it isn't easy to explain this. You'll want to know why I did nothing about them, when I knew that the Prefect has orders to hunt out all the Christians in this area. I find it difficult to understand myself, but I suppose I had several reasons. I had other more immediate practical things to do; it was an edict of the Emperor's that I did not agree with—I had a wound bound up once by a Christian surgeon and he was no enemy of the state; also I had myself taken a liking to the young man, Brychan. What I would have done if I had realised that you might become involved I don't know, though I think I was blind not to see that it might happen. Brychan has a rare quality that you don't meet very often in a place like Caer Taff. Fabius has it too, in a way, and you have hung about him since you were a small child. I should have foreseen that the same thing would happen over Brychan."

"But how did you know that Brychan was a Christian?" asked Con.

"Little things, he didn't really try to hide it. I've had some experience in being observant in that way. Now, Con, I want you to answer one question for me truthfully. Will you do that?"

"Yes, I'll try."

"Very well; last night you made me angry and I frightened you as a result. What was it you were really afraid of?"

"It's difficult," said Con slowly. "I thought you might beat me, and that wouldn't have been pleasant, so I suppose that was part of it; but really it was something else. I think I was frightened of myself—that you might make me tell about Brychan. I was so sure I had done what I had to do that I couldn't have forgiven myself if I'd betrayed him. That sounds very strange, but I think it's what I felt and you did ask me."

"The Gods be thanked then that Fabius was a good enough friend to seek me out and tell me what I needed to know. You have a lot to be grateful to him for, although this morning I was angry because he had put you into danger. Now I see that you were in it already, and it wasn't his fault. I would not have wanted to think less well of him. There was one other thing he told me that you will be glad to know. I think by now Brychan will have already moved from the hut where you left him, so you needn't be afraid that you will be forced to lead a squad of guardsmen back there. Fabius did not tell you the full plan that he had made for Brychan's escape."

Con took a deep breath and let it out in a sigh of relief. "Do you think they'll get away, Father?"

"It's quite likely. But we must get one thing clearly understood now, Con. Whatever has happened in the last few days and whatever are the rights and wrongs of it, the story will go on now without you. Do you realise how fortunate you've been? This was no boy's game you've been playing, it was an affair for the state, and one where you could have been swept past my reach to help you. I must warn you that if Brychan should come to Caer Taff again, or any other of his Christian friends, and I find out that you know about it, you'll be fighting me and the state together. Do you understand me?"

"Yes, I think so." Con's voice was flat.

Aemilius smiled at him. "This has been difficult for you, hasn't it? And I expect that one of the most puzzling things was that I wasn't crosser than I have been. You see, Con, I'm afraid you are learning now two lessons that I would rather you had found out in a different way; that Rome and the powers of Rome may seem both stupid and cruel, and that I can be puzzled myself and seem disloyal. Still, if you had come to me and told me about Brychan and we had both helped him to escape that would have been even more difficult. I might have done it, too, for the dedication that Brychan's beliefs have required of him is something that I can understand, although it's many years now since I made my own offering, and the way of Mithras is not easy to follow here in Caer Taff. So, Con, as you grow older you too will come to understand how one can be disillusioned and still faithful; it's part of growing up."

Con sniffed hard. "I'm sorry, it's just that I feel shaky suddenly. I suppose I'd better go to school now."

"Yes, I imagine you can find some excuse for not having been there this morning." Aemilius had a dry smile. "But Con, remember, this adventure is now over, and to make doubly sure it stays over I shall have to find some way to occupy you this summer away from Caer Taff."

Con found Julius sitting on a mounting block part of the way down the road beside the fort. "So you're all right," he said. "Thank goodness, I was afraid that your father had shut you up too."

Julius got up carefully. He was pale and looked as if he

had slept badly. "No, we got it over with last night. I'd for-gotten that Father had been out to dinner; he hadn't noticed a thing till he got back and missed me. I was getting worried though, when you didn't turn up this morning, but I didn't dare go to your house. Was it bad?"

"Yes, in a way, but it's over now. I'll tell you later. I say, Julius, are you really all right?"

He put a hand on Julius's shoulder. "More or less," said his friend, wincing and moving the hand away. "No, really Con, I've had as bad before, and it was worth it, wasn't it?"

"Yes, Father went to see Fabius this morning, and just now he threatened me with terrible things if I ever saw Brychan again. He kept saying it was all over as far as we were concerned, but Julius, he was so certain that now I'm beginning to wonder if it was himself he was trying to per-suade. I wonder if we've really seen the last of Brychan after all!"

9

The City of the Legions

Con sat hunched on his pony as if he was going to a funeral, not to Isca. School was over for the summer and Julius had been whisked off by his father to help in the warehouse. Usually Con would have been wildly excited at the prospect of a month at the base camp of the legion, but not this time. The two months since Brychan's escape had seemed unending, and he was restless in a way he did not understand.

Aemilius, riding beside him at the head of the small detachment from Caer Taff, understood very well what was going on in his son's mind. Next spring he would be old enough to enlist, but it seemed that the months till then would be difficult for Con. He wondered, for the first time, whether his son would make a good soldier; most of the practical skills he had or would learn quickly, but there was more to life in a legion than that. Anyway, this summer might decide the matter one way or the other. Let him see more of the life of a soldier at first hand; if the army was wrong for the boy it was better to find out now. He wanted him well clear of Caer Taff in any case, and as the Deisi threat now seemed to be over it would be difficult to keep an active boy shut up at home during the summer.

"Look, round the hill, you can see the smoke already," he said, pointing.

THE CITY OF THE LEGIONS

Con shook himself and sat upright. Now he was here he would have to be careful. He did not want to sulk in front of officers who might be important to him in a few months' time.

The road looped round below a wooded rise, crowned with the blurred lines of an earlier native fort, and past the mudflats of the tidal river. Isca lay ahead. First, as at home, came the town that had grown up round the camp, dominated by the high oval walls of the amphitheatre and the level area of the parade ground. Beyond that the great legionary headquarters smoked and rumbled in the late afternoon sun like a cauldron coming to the boil.

As they passed through the town and turned into the road which led from the river to the south-west gate they could already hear the sound of the army—the noise made by any great concourse of men going about the business of preparing for the evening meal. It was a sound of trumpets, and carts rattling over the rutted roads to the store-sheds, and snatches of song as men marched home to their barracks; of barking dogs, and a shout of laughter from a group off duty. Along the walls the sentries marched and wheeled, their spears and helmets flashing sparks of fire; behind them the cookhouses, built clear of the barrack blocks along the inner ramparts, smoked and smelled of dinner.

The drawbridge of the south-west gate crossed a deep ditch full of stinging nettles, broken pottery and rubbish. The horses' hooves rang hollow on the wood, Aemilius answered the challenge of the guard, and they rode out below the twin turrets of the gatehouse.

An orderly at Aemilius's bridle called up, "You men are billeted in the third block at the end of the western section, Centurion."

"Good, our old quarters." Aemilius turned his detachment

down the road that skirted the wall and ran to the western corner of the fort. The third barrack block faced inwards towards the fourth across an alley. Aemilius dismounted at the end and gave his horse to a groom. His second-in-command came up from the rear of the column.

"See the men into their billets, Quintus, and then report back to me," he said. "And Con, you'd better go with the horses so that you know how to find the horse lines again, then come back here."

Con left his pony with the others near the quarters of the cavalry wing attached to the legion, and made his way back across the camp past the Administration Hall. Only the knowledge that he did not yet have leave to wander about alone took him past the entrance.

He entered the officers' quarters at the end of the third block rather shyly. Quintus put his head out of the store-room door and said, "Your father's in the washroom at the end of the passage."

Con followed his direction down the narrow corridor past the open door through which he could see his father's great white cloak slung across a bed. Aemilius was washing his face in the stone basin in the corner of the wash-room. There was a good deal of water splashed over the concrete floor already and he was pouring more over the back of his neck. His voice was muffled.

"Is that you, Con? Throw me the towel."

Con found one behind the door, Aemilius dried himself vigorously and did up the neck of his tunic again. "That's better. I'll have a bath later if I can, but I must go and report now. Get yourself cleaned up and you can come with me. Your baggage is in the little room opposite mine."

Con unstrapped his saddle bag and found a clean tunic. He was lacing on his better sandals when his father came in, dressed again in his full uniform but carrying the bronze helmet with its horizontal horsehair plume.

"I hope this doesn't take long. I'm hungry and I must go to the staff mess afterwards. This reporting is only formal, though there are some other men I've got to see."

There was no time for Con to ask any questions as he followed his father to the Administration Hall. Aemilius passed the guards at the entrance with a crisp salute and strode across the courtyard, dotted at this time of day with little groups of officers. In the hall beyond he paused.

"I must report at the adjutant's office. Wait here, I won't be long." He disappeared into one of the rooms that lined the aisles of the hall.

Con stood quietly beside a pillar. This was the largest and most magnificent building he had ever been in; from the mosaic to the painted and coffered ceiling every part was more splendid and intricate than anything at Caer Taff. At the far end stood the legionary shrine with its statue of the Emperor and the dedications of generations of camp officers. Rome must be like this, a thousand halls and temples all as imposing—and as far from Isca to an ordinary soldier as the north star. Two centurions laughing together passed close beside him. The taller of the two, a man in his middle thirties with dark curly hair, looked casually at Con and then stopped.

"Constantine, son of Aemilius! Is your father here already? And it's hardly a month since he left last time. These re-enlisted officers have a grand life, come and go as they please!"

"Hullo, Casca," said Con. "I haven't seen you since last year."

"When is it that you join us? This is the son of my old centurion when I was with the scout boats," he said to the other man.

"I shan't be old enough to enlist till the spring, but it's holidays and Mother's tired of having me at home, so Father brought me with him."

"How is your lady mother? Do you know I taught this boy to swim?" said Casca to his friend. "Think of it, and look at the size of him now, it makes me feel old!"

"You old, Casca?" said Aemilius, coming up behind them. "You should settle down and found a family, that would make you young again."

He put an arm affectionately round the younger man's shoulders and they walked out together into the beginning of the sunset.

"Come over and eat with me," said Casca. "Your man won't have had time to do anything special. I'll send my orderly across to tell your optio—is it still Quintus?—where you are."

He was quartered in one of the newest blocks near the Via Praetoria. The mess-room in the officers' quarters was more spacious than the one in their own barracks. Casca waved an arm around him.

"Nice, isn't it? This row were the ones burnt down last winter. They're brand new now, nicely paved and with lovely clean plaster. There's an Italian in my century who used to be a house-painter; I'm thinking of having something pretty painted on the walls here. Nothing startling, no dancing girls—that'd look bad in a general inspection. Perhaps a nice quiet hunting scene."

Aemilius laughed and took off his cloak. "Life's good, is it, Casca? You're moving up, I see; fourth centurion of the second cohort! Do you ever miss the old days when you painted your face green and spent your time soaked to the skin on wet nights out in the channel?"

"They were good days, but after I lost those two fingers

when the pirates jumped us I knew it was time I left. You need two good hands in a boat. Still, I do miss the sea when the gulls fly inland. I'm glad then that Isca isn't on the coast."

He called for wine, and then the servant brought in the evening meal. It was good, the normal rations supplemented with cheese and salad and two unusually young hens. Aemilius put his knife down at last and pushed back his stool.

"That's better, thank you, Casca. I never expected to eat as well my first night in camp. Now tell me, what's all the news in Isca?"

Casca grinned and tilted his stool. "Oh, the usual—promotions, demotions. Quintilian of the third cohort fell off a horse and broke his neck two days ago. There seems to be some trouble up at Segontium. I hear they're reducing the garrison, sounds cockeyed to me. Oh, and the Governor's much delayed Commission to stamp out Christianity has arrived at last."

"Has it now?" commented Aemilius casually, putting down his cup. "And what, or who, does it consist of?"

"One Clodius Priscus, a most unpleasant civilian with extraordinary powers. The Tribune is far from pleased. He's had to turn over an office and a detachment of guard to him, and the man spends his time interrogating terrified farmers and market women."

"And are any of them Christians?"

"One or two, I believe. Anyway, the cells under the Quaestor's block are filling nicely, but I think it will be some time before we can have an execution in the arena that's worth watching."

"Casca, you're as bloodthirsty as ever!" said Aemilius, looking sideways at Con. But he was sitting playing with his knife as if Christians were no concern of his.

"That's what I'm paid to be," said Casca, laughing. "And this province is so peaceful now."

"You should live in Caer Taff!" Aemilius stood up. "Even Con has scars to prove that the garrison there earns its keep."

"Oh yes, your raid. You must tell me about that some time, Con. It was your first action, wasn't it?"

"We must go," said Aemilius. "Come on, Con. Do you know your way back? Don't wait up for me, I shall be late."

Con lay awake in his narrow room with the white plastered walls. It was the first night he had ever spent inside the camp and he lay listening to the sounds of the legion settling for the night. A door slammed farther down the block in the men's quarters, and a burst of laughter from one of the sleeping-rooms echoed back from the opposite barrack, but already a hush was falling. The challenge of the sentries meeting on the western turret came sharp and clear. Feet passed his door going towards the wash-room, then Quintus, the optio of his father's detachment, opened the door.

"All right, Con?"

"Yes, thank you, Father said he'd be late."

"I won't wait up, we'll be busy tomorrow. Goodnight."

The door closed. Con wondered what he would do with himself next day. Always before, his visits to Isca had been brief and he had stayed with friends in the town. He began to miss Julius. His mind went back to the meal with Casca, and the man Clodius Priscus, he wondered what he was like; it was difficult not to picture him as an imposing figure like the Tribune, but this man was a civilian. Anyway, Caer Taff and Isca were miles apart and Brychan would be far west among his own people by now.

A trumpet sounded across the camp and another, nearer, answered it: Lights Out. The clear notes died away into the dark bowl of the sky, across the clustered roofs and silent woods beyond, as they had done for more than two hundred years. The great camp, and Con with it, slept in security.

The next night Con was asleep even before the trumpet sounded. The confused thoughts of the evening before were buried deep under layers of exhaustion.

The morning had begun early with his father waking him in the first grey light of dawn.

"You remember the centurion you met last night, Casca's friend? He's in charge of the preliminary training for recruits for our cohort. I was talking to him after you went to bed and he's got a new batch of boys who only came in four days ago. He says you can go and learn some of the basic drill with them. It'll give you a good start next year."

"But is it really all right?" asked Con, getting up quickly and hunting for his sandals. "I mean, it's very kind of him, but won't I be in the way?"

"He wouldn't have suggested it if he thought that. Anyway, you probably know more already about general camp routine than most of them, and it'll help to toughen you up."

Con, half scared, half very excited, snatched some bread off the table in the mess-room as he passed it and went through the early morning bustle of the camp to the drill ground. Hours later he came back, aching all over, his hands blistered by the unaccustomed weapon drill. His father greeted him.

"What was it like?"

Con's eyes shone. "It was terrible for the first hour, but the others were nice to me. But, Father, the weight of a regulation shield! How do you ever carry it any distance, let alone fight at the same time?"

Aemilius laughed. "It's difficult to believe when you start, but it comes. One day all the equipment will stop being a burden and start being what it really is, designed for its purpose."

The next days passed very quickly. Con began to feel the results of hours of drill and exercises. He had never before eaten so much or slept so soundly. Caer Taff seemed far away, beyond the low hills he saw blurred with summer rain as he tramped through the mud on his first route march. The time lengthened and now the apples were nearly ripe on the fruit trees outside the camp and a smell of wet leaves in the morning air showed that it was nearly autumn.

A morning came when Con could no longer drill with the recruits. In a few days the Provincial Governor would visit Isca, and they had to rehearse their part in the military parade. He hung around the barracks, bored and bad-tempered, realising bitterly that the time for playing was over and it would be a long winter before he would have the right to join the recruits again.

His father came back at mid-day. "Letters from home," he said. "It seems that all's quiet to westward now. Oh, and here's something for you from Julius."

Con caught the small packet his father threw over to him, two folded sheets of parchment tied with a leather thong that looked as if it came from a pair of old sandals. He had never had a letter from Julius before. Back in his room he sat down on the narrow bed and undid the knots. The two sheets were cut from a larger one, and were covered on the back with tallies from Septimius's old stock-taking accounts. The pen had come through in places, which made Julius's writing hard to read.

Con read the letter through twice, smiling at the formal beginning, copied from models they used at school. Julius was well, so were his family and the household of Aemilius. He hoped Con and his father were too. Then the style changed; it had been dull in Caer Taff during the summer, Julius wrote, his father would be coming to Isca for the visit of the Provincial Governor and he had decided to bring his son with him.

Julius in Isca, that would be good. Con stopped reading and thought of all there would be to do and show him. Then he read the last paragraph. "We should arrive the day after you receive this, and will stay at the house of my father's friend, the merchant Quirinius."

The next afternoon he went to the place where the north-west road left the town. They would have to come this way and he wanted to see Julius even before he became involved in the hospitality of Quirinius. He had a long wait, although there was plenty of traffic on the road to watch; the town was filling fast, for the Governor was due next day and there was to be a holiday and a display in the amphitheatre. Already the grass around it was dotted with the stalls of the mountebanks and market people.

It was late afternoon when he saw Septimius riding ahead of one of his heavy wagons. Julius was sitting on the high seat beside the driver.

Con greeted Septimius and swung himself up beside his friend. "I thought you were never coming. Did you have trouble on the road?"

"The bridge back by the horse-ford is being mended and somebody's cart got stuck in the mud. I thought we should never get through," said Julius. "What have you been doing to get so brown?"

"Training," said Con, flexing his muscles.

They were among the houses now, turning down towards the merchant's house near the river. Suddenly Con realised that there was something wrong. Julius's face was pale and there were dark marks under his eyes.

Con looked across at the driver, swaying with the rhythm of the cart and fully occupied with avoiding the other traffic in the narrow street. "What is it?" he asked quietly.

Julius leaned nearer him. "We must talk, Con. Wait a minute, I'll speak to Father."

He slid down and ran ahead, but he was quickly back.

"Come on," he said. "Father says I can go off for an hour as long as I'm not too late for dinner. Where can we go?"

Somewhere private where we can talk, thought Con. Somewhere unlikely. "We'll go to the amphitheatre," he said.

Julius walked back with him towards the camp and across the open ground to the high oval of wood and stone that rose in front of the south-west wall of the fort. A detachment of men was fixing the flagpoles that crowned its encircling buttresses, but otherwise it was empty. They passed under the stone entrance arch and out of the growing confusion of the market outside. Above the containing wall the tiers of wooden seats rose high above them and the voices of the men working up against the sky came down to them. Two, carrying the last of the poles up from the arena, paused and stared, but Con waved and they turned to climb up the steep steps, apparently satisfied.

"That was lucky, they were men of Casca's century," said Con. "Come on up here."

They climbed high up on the southern side and sat down on a row of seats near the top, where they could see the camp and town together.

"Now, whatever's the matter?" Con asked. "As long as we keep our voices down we're as private as anywhere in Isca."

Julius, sitting with his hands clasped between his knees, raised a bleak face. "It's Brychan, he's been arrested."

"Brychan? How—when was it?"

"Five days ago, before I wrote to you. I don't know what I would have done if we hadn't been coming to Isca anyway, because I couldn't have put it in a letter."

"But, Julius, where is he? How did it happen?"

"Somewhere in a village near Nidum. Fabius found out from a man at the fort. It sounds as if Amphibalus was ill again and they had to shelter. I suppose someone got suspicious and told one of the patrols; they've been very active that way since you left."

"But what happened to Amphibalus?"

"He's dead, Con. Fabius thought that when the soldiers burst in suddenly his heart must have given out. I can't bear to think about it. He was so quiet that most of the time one hardly remembered he was there, but it was a sort of resting quiet, not a dull one."

"I know, like on that evening in the fisherman's hut." Con stopped talking, remembering the way the old priest had spoken to them that night, not being able to believe he was dead. Then he too tried to stop thinking because it hurt too much.

"Fabius found out by accident that Brychan had been taken, when he was brought to Caer Taff for questioning with some other prisoners," said Julius. "Isn't it strange, Con, there was that time when we were afraid that we might accidentally give him away, and now some other sort of accident has happened that we had nothing to do with."

"Have the prisoners only been questioned so far?"

Julius looked away. "Yes, I think so. But now they've been brought here to the special commissioner. You'll have heard of him."

"Clodius Priscus, yes indeed! But it's all been so quiet, Julius. I'd almost forgotten about it."

"The arrests must have been timed so that there would be some prisoners to produce for the Governor, when he comes. Look, I must go, but, Con, isn't there anything we can do? That's why I had to talk to you today. You know the camp, where's Brychan likely to be taken?"

Con looked over to the rows of barrack roofs and the portico of the Administration Hall; past it, farther on, was the punishment block. Perhaps Brychan would be there by now, brought in by another gate even as they sat there talking. He got up.

"We'll be chased out of here if we stay much longer, and your father will be cross. I've got to think, Julius, I can't believe all this yet. I'm fairly sure I know where Brychan will have been taken but I'll have to find out if I'm right."

He led the way back down to the road. "Look, you know your own way from here. Quirinius's house is that way. Meet me tomorrow, about the third hour, by the gate. Perhaps I'll have thought of a plan by then."

Julius squeezed his shoulder and turned away, but Con stood a little longer looking at the high gate and its twin towers.

That night he ate his meal quickly and went to bed. Aemilius cocked an eyebrow and asked, "Too many green apples, Con?" and he did not disagree.

Lying there in the cool, dim room he began to think. The way Julius had told of Brychan's capture had been more revealing than his actual words. He could see it so clearly. A ransacked hut with the spoiled clothes trailing among the broken pottery, and the body of an elderly man lying half out of a disordered bed. Then Brychan, a prisoner among tall legionaries; Fabius making his discreet enquiries among his friends in the bath-house.

Con wondered what the reward for informing against a

Christian was, and how it would feel to be the kind of person who could accept such money. He pushed away the memory of the desolation in Julius's eyes and tried to think constructively. He must find out before he met Julius again if Clodius Priscus was still using a room in the Quaestor's block, and if that was where Brychan had really been taken.

Then, when there was nothing more that he could plan until the morning, he had a sensation of desolation and emptiness; it seemed to have blanketed out all other feelings, and yet he was sure that from somewhere in the darkness a thought was trying to reach him. For a moment he was frightened, and longed for the comforting familiarity of Julius, then he thought that he understood.

Sliding out of bed he stood with his hands raised, as he had been taught to when he prayed. "God of Brychan, I don't understand what there is I can do, but if there is something, don't let me not do it because of my own stupidity. And God of Brychan, if you are a God of love as he says you are, be with him tonight, and with those in prison with him. Be with us all."

10

The Trumpets Sound

Con was late. Julius waited for him sitting on the edge of the water trough beside the drawbridge. It was going to be a lovely day. The first faint morning haze had gone and the sky was a darker blue than it had been all summer. He watched the flies buzz over some offal in the ditch; a wasp crawled on an apple core at his feet, and he squashed it viciously under his sandal. So much was beautiful, the day, the lines of men drilling on the parade ground, and yet the bitterness in his heart was poisoning everything.

He slid down to the ground as Con came out from the shadow of the archway, spoke to the guard, and waved him across. Selfconsciously, almost as if he were the prisoner, he crossed the bridge and followed Con into the camp.

"Come on," said Con. "No time to show you anything now, I've got a lot to tell you."

It was quiet in the officers' block. The men were all away, and the orderly marking lists on the messroom table only raised his head when Con led the way down the passage to his room. Once there he closed the shutter carefully and perched himself on the one stool. Julius sat on the bed looking at him.

"Tell me what you found out," he said. "I can see something's happened."

"First of all, Brychan. He came last night just before the gate closed. I was talking to Casca and I didn't even have to ask him! He was outside the Quaestor's block, absolutely furious. It seems that now there are some extra prisoners, Priscus has asked for more guards to look after them. Some of Casca's men had been detailed and that would have meant their missing the parade when the Governor arrives this evening. Casca had just been having a row about it. He said he couldn't spare the men till afterwards."

"So that means the prisoners will be less heavily guarded till then," said Julius.

"Just so, and not only that. I thought when Casca told me all this that Priscus would have to keep them in the cells today, but not a bit of it. He wants some confessions, and he hasn't had the chance to examine Brychan and the others who came in yesterday yet, so he's going to carry on as usual."

"Twice the prisoners and half the guards! But still, he won't take them out of the Quaestor's block, and we can't get in," said Julius.

"Not at the moment, but I've got the beginnings of an idea. Listen, I'll tell you what the block's like. There's an entrance with a guard-room on either side, and behind that a small yard. The offices are round the sides and there's another guard-room at the back on the right. The steps down to the cells are in there. Priscus is using a room on the right-hand side. Casca told me that the Quaestor's fairly annoyed about it too. He's short of space as it is, and he's got to find room now for some of the Governor's secretariat. Priscus hasn't made himself very popular, Casca says, and for two pins the Quaestor would have him moved out altogether for the next few days. There's a room quite near he could have; it's in the hospital next door and there's been some trouble with a drain that was blocked up, so it's rather smelly and not being used."

"So if for some reason Priscus could be prevented from using his own room, then the prisoners would have to be taken backwards and forwards to the hospital for questioning, and they're likely to be more lightly guarded than usual," said Julius. "It sounds like a lot of ifs, and how could we possibly arrange for the room to be out of use?"

There was silence. A fly buzzed against the shutters, and outside a man called across to a friend. Then Julius raised his head.

"Wasps," he said.

"What?"

"Wasps. I've been thinking, does Priscus's room have an outside window?"

"Yes," said Con, "a small one on to the alley that leads past the hospital. It's part of the oldest section of the camp and the space between the buildings is more cramped over there."

"Then that's perfect. Don't you see? I've been thinking of all the things that would stop Priscus using the room. We can't get into it through the door, and if we put something that smelled in through the window, or tried to set fire to it then someone would be suspicious. But wasps could happen to anyone, and if there were enough the room would be unusable."

"But where would they come from?" asked Con, still puzzled.

"There's a wasp's nest under the bridge, I saw it when I was waiting for you. I don't mind them, we get a lot in the warehouse; the stings hurt, but they don't swell up on me. Con, say we got hold of something sweet and sticky and spilled it just below Priscus's window. If there was no one in the room at the time we might even get some inside as well. Then if I can get hold of part of that wasp's nest and let some loose I don't think Priscus would be there for long."

Con started to laugh. The stool rocked and he nearly fell off. "Julius, it's marvellous, and like all good plans, it's simple. Wait a minute, though, how can you get the wasps?"

"If I dropped something into the ditch by mistake would the guard let me go down to get it?" asked Julius.

"Yes. I should think so. Oh, I see, while you're hunting about under the bridge you get the nest into some sort of a bag. I'm glad it's going to be you doing that! Wait a minute though, then what happens? Say we can use the wasps about mid-day when it's likely to be quiet and the room may be empty; we shall just have to hope that Priscus needs to interrogate Brychan after that. I don't think he will be finding Brychan easy to question, though, and he's likely to have to see him more than once. Oh, Julius . . ."

"Stop it, there's no sense in thinking about that side of it when there are things we can do. Now, what happens next?"

"Several more of your ifs. But somehow I think the Governor himself may help us later this afternoon. He's supposed to be arriving an hour before sunset. There will be a ceremonial procession up to the Administration Hall and everyone who isn't on duty will be lining the Via Principalis or cheering in the crowd. The rest of the camp will be deserted; that would be the time. There are two of us and not likely to be more than two guards, who wouldn't be expecting trouble. But where could Brychan go if we got him away from the fort?"

"To the store behind Quirinius's house, and then westward if possible," said Julius. "That's where he'd be safest in the end, but the heaviest guard would be on that road."

"Not necessarily," said Con. "It might be too obvious. I'm

sure Fabius would help again if we could once get Brychan to Caer Taff. I wish he was here now. Getting out of the camp in the first place won't be easy, and it's something we can't plan till we see how things go."

"There'll be the crowds moving in and out at sunset."

"Yes, you're right. A lot of officers live in the town or have wives there; they'll be taking them back after the parade's dismissed."

"If you can get Brychan as far as that I should be able to manage the rest and then your father won't have to know anything about it," said Julius. "Mine won't miss me for ages, or I might even be able to work out an acceptable excuse for going back to Caer Taff in a hurry."

"I suppose that's as far as we can get, now." Con's flow of invention suddenly dried up and he began to look worried.

Julius said, "Yes, but only let us get so far and Brychan will be free, Con. I have a feeling that it's all going to work."

Con looked across at him, but there did not seem to be anything else to say. He got up and rummaged among his things for a skin food-bag. "Would this do for you?"

Julius tested the draw-string at the neck. "Yes, that's perfect, it pulls tight. I don't want to leak wasps all over the camp, they're going to be very cross. What will you do now?"

"I'm going back to the prison block to see if I can find out any more about what Priscus is doing. Then I'll get something sticky from the cook-house."

"Be careful not to hang about too much near the prison, the guards might recognise you."

Con grinned. "They change at mid-day, you know. Come on, we'll have to be quick. I'll see you back to the gate."

They walked back, trying not to hurry too obviously. Julius looked towards the Via Principalis, where the garlands were fluttering in the light breeze. On any other day it would

have been fun to explore the camp, but not today. It had become a hostile place not an exciting playground. There was
time now for only one thing, not even the time to be frightened.
He went on ahead while Con talked to the gate guard, and
sat down on the low rail of the bridge, swinging his legs. He
started to fiddle with his knife, and did not look up as Con
came up to him.

"Ready?"

Julius started convincingly, and dropped the dagger.

"Bother," he said. "Can I go down and get it?"

The guard waved him on and he slipped down into the
stinging nettles under the bridge.

Con left him there and made his way across the camp and
up past the grain-stores to the hospital block. It was built
on the usual camp pattern round a courtyard, but it was an
old building and generations of camp surgeons had added to
it. For part of its length the lane which divided it from the
prison block had been halved in width by a row of lean-to
store-rooms. The door of the empty room opened outwards
just where the lane widened again. Con shifted his attention
to the other wall, there was nothing much to see. The grat-
ings from the underground cells opened inwards towards the
courtyard just above ground level, so he counted the windows of the rooms. The one that must belong to Priscus's
room was small and square with its shutter hooked back to
let in the light. It was high up, but the wall was roughly
built and would give toe-holds.

Con kicked at his sandal till the tie came loose. He knelt
down to fasten it again. There were men talking inside, close
above him. He listened carefully; one voice was loud and
official, was it Clodius Priscus? Something told him it was
not. This voice seemed to be trying to explain something;
another answered it, quiet, high, and much easier to hear.

"Very well, that will do. Now, man, how do you explain all this?"

There was a pause. Silence in the room. Then the answer came very low.

"I don't explain it." It was Brychan.

Con's fingers were trembling so much that now he could not have fastened his sandal if he had wanted to. If only no one would pass while he listened to what happened next.

"You must answer my questions," said the voice of Clodius Priscus.

Again there was silence. Then the louder voice was raised and there was the sound of a blow.

"Be still. Prisoner, do you intend to answer me?"

"No, sir."

"Very well, we will give you longer, a very little longer, to consider what you are saying. Take him away, I'll see him again later this afternoon."

Con got up shakily; so he had been right and Brychan was indeed proving difficult to interrogate. Round the corner, in the wider road that ran in front of the building, two guards were leaning against their spears in the entrance to the inner courtyard. The officer must be out of sight. One guard, short and dark, turned towards him.

"Aaron!" said Con. "Aaron from Father's boat, the only Hebrew who ever went to sea! Whatever are you doing stuck over here?"

The wide mouth under the hooked nose split into a smile. "Keep an eye on the guard-room door," he said to the other guard. "Well, if it isn't Constantine! I heard you were here with your father. I've not been too lucky since I got the injury that took me off the scout boats. And now I'm on guard duty today of all days!"

Con leaned against the wall here he could see across the

courtyard to the door of Priscus's room. This was luck
undreamed of; he had known Aaron ever since he could
remember. Everything was going well.

"I'm sorry to hear that," he said. "Does your leg bother
you much? And how do you come to be on duty today?"

"Oh, you know how it is. We're short-handed and they
had to choose out the pretty boys for the parade, and that's
something I've never been."

"When do you come off duty?" asked Con. The door of
the room was opening.

"Not till after the parade, though we shall get a bit of
relief at mid-day. This isn't a job I like at all." Con thought
there was something queer about that, but there was no
time to follow it up.

"Watch it," hissed the other guard.

Aaron straightened up and Con melted away across the
road as the sergeant of the guard came out followed by a
short thin man in a toga. Con only had time to wink at his
friend before he wandered on. So that was Clodius Priscus,
the man who was the enemy. He had not seen him closely,
but the undersized, almost sickly body had surprised him,
and the curiously pale face under the thatch of faded hair.
And Con had a memory, which he could not pin down to
any one detail, of extraordinary coldness.

By the time he got back to his room Julius was already
there, sitting down with one hand round the neck of a bag
that buzzed and heaved, while he sucked the other.

"What on earth have you got there?" he asked Con.
"Grapes?"

"No, figs. Wait while I get something to put them in."

He found an earthenware bowl in the wash-room and
poured the sticky pile on to it from a cabbage leaf. The figs
oozed juicily as he stirred them.

"There, I think those look very waspy," he said. "And I got some honey as well, in case there's a chance to use it."

Then he told Julius all he had heard. "It's almost mid-day now," he finished. "We must make this squashy mess a bit tidier and then go back before Priscus uses the room again; and Father may be back at any moment."

"Wait, let's go through what we're going to do once more," said Julius. "This is all happening so quickly that I'm afraid we shall make some silly mistake."

"I scout ahead; when it's clear I spill the figs and the honey." Con ticked off the points on his fingers. "Then I signal to you and you bring the wasps. After that all we can do is wait."

"That was what was worrying me, I knew there was something," said Julius, twisting the bag of wasps in a worried way. "How are we going to know what happens then—if the room really is changed? We shall have to stay and watch all the time. Didn't you say there were some low buildings next to the hospital? Would it be possible for someone to hide on the roof of one of them, and stay there all afternoon?"

"I suppose so, and there might be room for both of us. Wait a minute, though, if we could jump down on the guards from above we should have a much better chance than if we just rushed out from behind a corner."

"And we wouldn't need to use any weapons. Brychan wouldn't want that, he'd rather go on being a prisoner than have us hurt anybody."

"Yes, I hadn't thought of that, but I'm going to take something to hit with, just in case."

Con looked about the room. One of the legs of his stool had been loose for some time. He twisted it away from the seat and stowed it in the top fold of his tunic.

"Right, now come on!"

Once they were clear of the barracks Con went on ahead. Already far more civilians than usual were in the camp and Julius passed unnoticed. They paused at the back of the hospital block, where they could just see down the narrow alley between the buildings. Con disappeared but was quickly back, signalling from the other end.

As he reached Priscus's room all was still quiet. He uncovered the bowl and the oozing greeny-purple mess of split figs slid out at the foot of the wall. He picked up a handful of it and smeared it higher.

Then he got a toe-hold and hoisted himself carefully to the level of the window-sill. There was no one there. He slid down and found a fig that still seemed fairly firm and leaned back inside the window. There was a faint clatter and then he took the little jar of honey from the wallet at his belt. Some went inside and some trickled unobtrusively between the joints of the stone below the sill. Finally he jumped down and signalled to Julius.

"Priscus will never want to see a wasp again. Neither do I," said Julius as he caught up with him round the corner. "What did you do inside the room, Con? They found it straight away."

"There was a cup of wine on the table. I knocked it over with a fig. It's all right, it rolled away and I don't think anyone will find it. When I'd spilt the honey too it was a horrid sticky mess, but it looked natural. Now all we can do is wait. Let's have a look at that roof. Thank goodness there's no one about."

The corner of the outbuilding stuck out a little way past the window. It was roughly built of wood, and Julius climbed up quickly and disappeared on to the top. After a moment he stuck his head over again.

"This is perfect, the roof sags right down and it isn't overlooked."

Con looked at the bowl he was still carrying. There seemed nowhere to hide it, so he climbed up to the roof still holding it.

Five hours later the high blue sky was beginning to cloud over. The great camp lay quiet, except along the decorated processional way. Two hours after mid-day there had been consternation and disturbance in the prison block, and Priscus—complaining bitterly—had transferred his papers to the other room. So far two prisoners had been taken there, but not Brychan.

From far down towards the river there was the sound of cheering. "Surely they've gone for Brychan this time," whispered Julius.

In the prison block a door slammed and there was the sound of marching feet. Con's hand closed round the stool leg and he crouched ready, his tunic hitched out of the way. Julius's hand caught at his shoulder, pulling him lower as the feet turned the corner behind them. Julius scooped up a handful of dust and dry moss from the gutter. For a moment their eyes met, aware for the first time of the impossible thing they were going to do.

Then the soldiers were below them. Con jumped on to the back of the nearest, Julius threw his dust into the face of the other and jumped himself, rolling like a cat to get on top. Con's man seemed to be shouting, but all he could see from the ground was a confusion of dust and flying feet. He choked and spat, then suddenly the soldier's hold on him slackened. Julius caught at his arm.

"Quick, the others!"

The door of Priscus's room flew open and the officer ran out. Con found himself on his feet, seeing in one brief moment a crumpled man on the worn stones and Julius flying down the alley away from him. Brychan was standing looking at the cut ends of the ropes that had bound him. Con grabbed his arm and dragged him back round the corner towards the prison.

Now there was only running, and feet pounding behind as they doubled back along the front of the hospital. No time to wonder where Julius had gone, only to hope he was getting away. Then even that thought was lost in the terror of hunted things.

Con turned right, then right again. Not far ahead was the sound of cheering, and the clatter of horses' hooves, suddenly very loud. Brychan was sobbing for breath, stiff and weakened by his imprisonment. The men behind them shouted, and a guard ahead turned, left his post, and barred their way with a spear.

Con pushed Brychan through the nearest doorway. It was the entrance to the compound where the grain was stored. In ten paces they were out of sight behind the great storage

I 129

bins. The wall at the back brought them up short, and already the hunt behind was shouting in the doorway, but beyond the wall and to the right were the heads of the crowd and the spear points of the men lining the route.

"Only one jump, Brychan!" Con pushed the exhausted man up from behind and leapt for the top of the wall. He rolled over and landed in a heap behind the backs of a crowd of men off duty, jamming the side turning which led to the main road.

The cheering rose to a climax, and with a clatter of iron on stone the Governor's chariot rolled slowly past. Con and Brychan, working their way deeply into the crowd, saw a glimpse of a pale, remote profile and a wreath of gold, and then the crowd surged forward again.

Con put an arm round Brychan's shoulders. He had to shout into his ear to make himself heard. "Now for the main gate!"

11

"God of Brychan"

The crowd began to break up as soon as the Governor had passed. Men were looking at the sky and pulling their cloaks around them. Suddenly the sound of the trumpets farther up the route of the procession was drowned by a peal of thunder. Con and Brychan crossed the dangerous width of the Via Principalis hurrying at the heels of a family group, and then checked a moment to look at the sky as the first big raindrops fell on the warm paving stones.

There was no sign that the hunt was still after them as they approached the western gate, for the crowd was making any movement difficult inside the camp. The rain grew heavier, the shoulders of their tunics were soaked and their hair, dark and wet, hung over their eyes. Con looked at Brychan.

"No one would recognise you now. We must get through those gates before anyone sounds a general alarm, and then to Quirinius's warehouse."

"But what happened to Julius?" Brychan seemed slowly to be becoming less dazed now he had his breath back, but he looked very worried.

Con had not had time himself to wonder about that, but he said, "We'll see him there, I expect. He knows where we are going. He'll join us later."

They pressed on, splashing through the puddles. Twilight

seemed to be coming early with the storm and it was almost dusk. The thunder rumbled again as the high towers of the gatehouse loomed over the huddled backs of the hurrying groups ahead. The drawbridge echoed under their feet, and they were out between the market stalls that now edged the road to the town. Con turned off down a side street that led towards the river.

The warehouse backed on to the quay where iron ore from inland was loaded to be shipped down river to the estuary; now two small cargo boats were moored there, already loaded with empty oil jars. In the murky light no one saw them as they slipped through the wide entrance behind an empty wagon and climbed the ladder to the loft above Quirinius's main store. There, well hidden behind the sacks and bundles, they sank into a pile of loose straw in the mouse-smelling darkness.

For a little while, until the thundering of his heart had steadied and he had wrung some of the water out of his tunic, Con said nothing. Then he crawled carefully to the edge of the loft floor and looked down into the open space below. There was no one about and he came back to Brychan.

"Julius should be here by now. I don't understand why he's so long."

"There's a lot I wish you had time to tell me," said Brychan. "But, Con, shouldn't you get back to the fort? I suppose your father's there and he'll miss you."

"Not for some time yet, he's on duty, but I must get back before the gates close or I shall be in trouble."

"How did you know what had happened?"

"Fabius found out. Brychan, we're going to try to get you back to him; he's the only person we can think of who can help you now."

"But half the legion will be on the road to Caer Taff."

"Then we mustn't use the road. Those boats outside, I know them, they trade up and down the coast all the time with oil and wine and local things. With any luck they're waiting for the morning tide now. Tell Julius what I said when he comes; he might be able to get you on board one before dawn."

Brychan hardly seemed to be listening. "How is it that it was so easy?" he said, almost to himself. "It was a soldier who cut my hands loose. I don't understand."

Con turned to him, startled. "What did you say?"

"Didn't you see? No, I suppose you were rolling on the ground with the other man; but the guard who held me rubbed the dust from his eyes and drew his knife. I thought he was going to kill me, but he cut the ropes round my wrists, kicked the man on the ground, and hauled you up by your belt. Don't you remember?"

"Yes, I do now, but it was all so mixed up. Where was Julius?"

"I didn't see him at first, but he ran away up the alley after the officer came out of the interrogation room." Then he added very quietly, "I'm afraid of a second Verulamium."

Con did not hear that. He was peering through the gloom trying to see the priest's face; he still seemed very strange.

"Brychan, will you be all right? He's sure to come soon, and later on you should be able to climb down and find something to eat. Tell Julius that if I can I'll get back as soon as the gates are open. Why does there always seem to be a storm when we meet you?"

He climbed quickly down the ladder. The last western rays of the sun were shining yellow from under the rim of the dark storm-clouds as he reached the main road to the camp. They faded as it dipped behind the black hills and he began to run again. The gates were just closing as the last stragglers who lived in the town hurried across the bridge.

Once he was safely through he put his head down and hurried towards the barracks, keeping close against the wall, hoping he would see no one he knew. The mess-room and the passage beyond it were empty as he passed through them. He closed his own door carefully and sat on the bed, slowly drying his hair with a towel. Outside the rain trickled from the gutters and ran in rivulets between the rows of barracks. It was dark, but he did not light the lamp. He was tired, and a little cold, but apart from that he did not feel anything very much. There was nothing else to do tonight and he was numb inside after the intensity of the last hours, except for a vague concern about Julius.

The main door of the officers' quarters slammed. Con heard voices; he got up slowly, shivering a little, and lit the lamp. His father's footsteps sounded in the passage and the door opened.

The centurion was still wearing his ceremonial armour, the polished bronze clouded by the rain. He stood in the doorway unfastening his helmet, then he came right into the room, put it down on the table and shut the door. Con got up and stood facing him.

"Constantine, did you know that Brychan was in the fort being questioned?"

"Yes, Father."

"Did you also know that he escaped two hours ago?"

Con dropped his eyes and said nothing. He was more frightened now than he had been up on the roof before the jump.

Aemilius lifted the small lamp from the table and looked around him, then he stooped to pick up something from the floor. Con's eyes, following his hand, saw that it was a fig.

Aemilius put it down and turned back to him.

"Con, look at me. Did you help Brychan to escape?"

The boy raised his eyes, took a deep breath and let it go again, then he said in a small voice that he did not recognise himself, "Yes, Father."

Then Aemilius was angry. Con saw the flush spread over his face and stepped back involuntarily, but his father's voice was quiet too.

"Do you have any idea of the appalling thing that you have done to yourself and the whole family? I warned you what would happen if anything like this should occur again, but it never entered my head even then that you would do anything as criminally reckless as this. I must decide what to do with you, but meanwhile there is one thing I need not delay. Take your tunic off. This time I'm going to give you the beating of your life."

Con, loosing the buckle of his belt, his back to the door, heard his father go to his own room; then he came back and slammed the door to behind him. Con wondered if it was going to be the ceremonial cane or the riding whip. Nothing happened. He shivered a little in the rain-cooled air, watching a trickle of water run down the plaster from the window-sill, and jumped when his father spoke at last.

"No, I've never beaten you in hot blood before, and I can't do it now. I'll come to you again later."

The door closed. Con listened for the bolt to fasten on the outside but his father did not pause at all. Slowly he pulled a blanket from the bed and wrapped it round his body; then he lay down with his face pressed into the pillow by the wall. After a while he began to cry in an unpractised way.

Hours later, long after the evening trumpet, his father came in again. Con, still awake with his thoughts, did not move. Aemilius sat down on the edge of the bed.

"Con, we've got to have a talk together."

The boy twisted round and sat up in bed, pulling the blanket round him. Aemilius was magnificent in his best uniform and gilded sandals. Con remembered the Governor; there would have been a dinner at headquarters.

Aemilius looked at his son with a mixture of compassion and exasperation, the anger quite gone. "Con, a boy who I think must be Julius has been arrested. Brychan seems to have got clean out of the camp, but I expect you know that. Julius would appear to have been taken in mistake for him."

"Father, where is he?"

"He was taken back to the Quaestor's block and he's being questioned now. I don't know anything else except that Aaron the Hebrew, the man who used to be on my boat, was arrested too."

Con remembered the running figure he had seen just before he escaped himself. "Julius has red hair and a brown tunic, like Brychan, and I think his weak leg got stiff up on the roof, perhaps he couldn't run very fast. Oh, what a horrible mess. What will happen to him? He won't be hurt, will he?"

"Con, I think you'd better tell me exactly what happened."

Con did not answer straight away. He looked at his father, his hands clasped round his knees. It was chilly in the little room; Aemilius got up and threw a cloak about his son's bare shoulders. From behind Con, out of sight of the puzzled eyes, he said, "Con, you must trust me this time. You understand, don't you, that it's not just a question of Julius? You are still in danger yourself, and the rest of the family through you. I know I frightened you before and you thought I might make you betray Brychan to the authorities. Now we are all of us in danger. Brychan himself wouldn't want anyone to be hurt if there was no need."

"I suppose you're right. Anyway, I can't decide what to do on my own any longer."

Con told Aemilius what had happened during the last day. When he had finished his father sat silent, looking at the bright flame of the lamp.

"It happened so quickly," said Con. "There wasn't time to think as far ahead as what would happen now. I suppose we behaved like children playing a game. We were trying to save Brychan's life because we thought it wasn't fair that he should suffer, but we never dreamed that one of us might be arrested in his place. I know you warned me, but when it all happened yesterday that didn't seem important."

"And now Julius stands before Clodius Priscus, and what is he going to tell him? What will he be strong enough to conceal? Will the guards be coming for you, or knocking on the door of Quirinius the merchant before the night is out?" said Aemilius.

*   *   *   *

The lamp on its high stand threw a pool of light downwards. Julius blinked as he tried to see past it to the rest of the room.

"If you had nothing to hide why were you running away?" asked the quiet, dry voice again.

"I thought I had strayed into a part of the camp where I shouldn't have been, and I was frightened." If only there were more time to think ahead, to plan answers to the questions that would surely come.

"Why were you frightened?"

"I don't know, I just was."

"How did you come to be in the camp at all?"

This was getting more and more difficult. "I came to see the Governor."

"And did you come alone?"

"Yes."

"Come, is that likely? A boy who does not know the camp and is frightened by a few soldiers running?" Clodius Priscus leaned forward into the circle of light. His face was oval, pale under pale hair. Julius noticed his mouth for the first time, the upper lip came down into a little point at the middle; when he was not speaking it shut as precisely as a locked door.

"No," said Julius. "I was alone, that's why I was frightened."

"What is your name?" The question was quick and suddenly loud.

Julius said nothing.

"Where do you live?" There was a little pause.

Again silence. Suddenly one of the guards who had him by the shoulders struck Julius across the side of the head. He swayed, held upright in their arms.

"What is your full name?" Again silence followed by a blow.

Julius began to cry very softly. It was no use, there was nothing else he could say without putting Con and his own father in danger. Better to stop now, to say nothing if only that were possible. He shut his eyes, trying to blot out the little room, and Isca, and all the power of the Province of Britain. A tiny clear picture flashed before his eyes of Brychan kneeling in the firelight of the fisherman's hut the night Amphibalus had told them the story of Albanus.

A hand pulled his head back and he opened his eyes involuntarily. Clodius Priscus was standing up now; he looked a little annoyed, but with the irritation of a man whose sandal strap has broken. Julius realised that was why he was so frightening—people were no more than things that could be awkward or co-operative. Had he never been happy or afraid himself, so that he did not understand what emotions meant to other people?

"Take him down to the cells, I'll see him again at dawn. He knows a little, I think, what will happen to him then," he said.

The rain was pouring down again out of the blackness as the guards splashed back into the prison courtyard. A light burned in the guard-room above the cells, but the stone steps were wet and badly lit and Julius stumbled as he turned the corner at the bottom. There was no light at all down here except from the torch carried by the man ahead. He stopped and swung down the wooden beam across one metal-studded door, and the second guard pushed Julius through. The door slammed behind him, leaving him in complete darkness.

He stayed quite still, pressing back against the rough planks, trying to see where he was, till a voice called up from below, "There are six steps. The wall's on your left. Watch out, they're slippery."

Julius's hand touched the wet stone. "Who are you?" he asked. "Is there anyone else there?"

"No, only us. Come on down, the straw's fairly dry." The voice was friendly, with a hint of an accent he could not place.

"What's your name?" Julius asked again, as he felt his way down the steps. "I'm Julius."

"They call me Aaron the Hebrew. If you're who I think you are you've seen me before this evening. You threw dust in my eyes. Come over here. I can't come to you, they've chained me up."

Julius felt his way through the straw. This man sounded as if being chained up in prison was the most natural way there was of spending the night, he thought. A little of the fear left him as his hand touched the man's arm.

Aaron's hand found his and pulled him down to where he was sitting on a pile of straw with his back to the wall. The hand felt his hair and wet tunic.

"So it's still raining. Boy, you're shivering. Come close to me, then we can keep each other warm."

Julius leaned his aching head back against the wall. "What are you doing here?" he asked.

"Didn't you see? I helped a prisoner to escape."

"But why did you do it? I don't understand. You've been on guard duty all day, why did you suddenly help us to get Brychan away?"

"Was that his name? I didn't even know that. It's a long story, it goes back more than seven years, I think. This isn't the first time I've guarded Christians you see."

Julius wished that he could see the man's face; he had only seen him for a moment as he walked past the Quaestor's block, but he began to have an idea what might be behind Aaron's behaviour.

140

"You weren't stationed at Verulamium, were you?"

The man shifted beside him in the straw, rubbing his ankles where the heavy shackle rested on them. "So you know that story, do you? Yes, I saw Albanus die, and he didn't die alone. It was one of my friends who should have done it; Albanus was a soldier, you see, and had the right to be beheaded. When it came to the point my friend wouldn't do it, so they cut him down on the spot—to preserve discipline! Then they found someone who would, and all the while I was standing there sweating because I was next in line, and if he'd refused it would have come to me. And there was something about the two of them, I was so close I could see the way they looked. It came between me and my rest every night till I knew that look had been meant as much for me as anyone else. I sniffed out some of their people and found out what made them like that."

"Aaron, are you a Christian?"

"Yes and no, I was at first. Some Christians don't hold with being in the army, but the brothers at Verulamium weren't strict about that as we were only on garrison duty and there wasn't any fighting; then they might have worried. Still, I had to wait for baptism right round until the next spring, and the water was hardly dry on me when I was posted back to the ships. Then it wasn't easy. There were very few of the brethren near Caer Taff and I could never get to be with them. I don't know how much you know about it, but if you follow our Master it's very hard on your own; being a Christian is meant to be a thing you share with other people. Away from my friends I was like a coal taken from the fire, the glow went out. I even began to forget Albanus. So there I was three days ago suddenly detailed to extra guard duty and without the strength to do anything about it."

"I'm sorry about the dust," said Julius. "We didn't know. But, Aaron, if you hadn't helped us I don't think Brychan would have got away, and he must have done or we would have heard them bringing him back."

"He was a priest, wasn't he?"

"Yes, it's strange you two should come together like that." Julius told him the story of Amphibalus.

"No, it's not strange," said Aaron when he had finished. "It's the way things work out for you when you're a Christian."

"Do you mean that you aren't free—that God meant you and me to be arrested instead of Brychan?"

"I'm not good at explaining things, but look, it's a bit like this. Our Lord didn't decide before I was born that he wanted someone to die tomorrow in Isca, nor did he mean you to be arrested, but somehow he could use your wanting to help Brychan, and even that you've got red hair. Things don't *have* to happen, it's just that looking back at them afterwards you can see a shape behind them."

"Aaron, are we going to die?"

"I think I am, and I suppose I knew it even when I was slogging my poor mate. It was just that something else seemed more important."

Julius was silent, shivering in the damp darkness. Aaron felt the movement and put his arm round him.

"It's late, you ought to try to sleep." Then, more quietly, "Did they hurt you, boy?"

"Not much, my head aches a bit, but I don't think I could sleep yet. Aaron, I'm not a Christian, I don't even know much about what your God is like. I only met Brychan a few times, and we didn't help him to escape because he was a priest but because we liked him."

"Wouldn't you think the kind of person he was depended

on his being a Christian? But how did he come to be taken?"

Julius explained that, and then he went back and told him all that had happened since the raid early in the spring. After that they sat in silence for a while. The stillness pressed down heavily, like the weight of stone in the building above them. Then Julius said, "Aaron, I want to ask you something; will you tell me the truth?"

"What is it?"

"What will happen to me in the morning? It's not knowing that's so bad."

"Tell me how old you are?"

"Just sixteen."

"And your father will be a respected citizen?"

"Yes, he's a merchant."

"Julius, if you had done anything except helping a Christian to escape I don't think anything much would have happened to you. As it is, Clodius Priscus will ask you questions again. He will want the names of all those who helped you, and he will use force to get them. Even if you tell him what he wants you will have to offer incense to the statue of the Emperor as if you were swearing the new year oath of loyalty. If you refuse to do that I think you will be condemned to death; for any other crime you're on the young side, but Christians must be stamped out from the cradle upwards." For the first time his voice was bitter.

"I suppose if I don't tell about the others at first that will help?" said Julius very quietly, almost to himself. "Aaron, tell me about your baptism. What does it mean, and do people always have to wait a long time for it? Must it be done by a priest?"

"No, any Christian can baptise, and it's not how long it takes to learn that's important, it's believing the right things. If it's not possible to go down to a river we use whatever water we can, there doesn't have to be much. It's only a sign to show that the old part of us has been drowned and we've come back to life as new people."

"That's rather difficult. Brychan said that being a Christian was finding out that there was a God who loved you and learning to love him back. I don't know your God, but I know Brychan and I believe in him—that anything he thinks is worth dying for must be true."

"Then you're very near us."

"But am I near enough? You see, I don't think I've got any more time. Even if I'm not a proper Christian I'm not going to burn that incense. Aaron, could you baptise me now?"

Aaron said, "Feel over to your right. Is there some water left in the jug?"

Julius tipped it. "Yes, but not much."

"As long as there's a few drops. Now, if these chains will let me I'd rather kneel while I say a prayer for us both. I wish your Brychan was here, but he isn't, so I must do the best I can."

When it was over Julius gave a little sigh. "What time do you think it is now? Do you know, I'm actually sleepy, and I want to be able to think clearly tomorrow."

"I think it's tomorrow already, it's well after midnight, but there's another five hours till dawn. Sleep well, Brother Julius."

As the boy's breathing became more regular Aaron settled him more comfortably across his knees and leant back. Perhaps this would be his last night on earth and he had a lot to think about. There was Albanus, and the young priest Brychan, and the memory of his own baptism. Most people had only their lives to serve God with, but he was going to

144

use his death, like his friend in Verulamium. It was a second
chance, really. Funny how now it came to it that was more
important than what would happen, perhaps tomorrow, in
the arena outside the fortress walls. Then he thought about
Julius, and after a while he prayed.

He woke him as the dawn cocks were crowing. Even here
the sound came faintly down from the grating high up on the
wall. Already the darkness was less. As the boy sat up he
could see the grey shape of the man at last.

Aaron stretched his legs. "It was a shame to wake you,
but there's movement upstairs; I think they'll come for you
soon."

"What about you?" Julius tried to get his mind clear,
he felt chilled and dizzy and there was a bitter taste in his
mouth.

"There's only one end to what I started yesterday. They
won't have me out till later, when they charge me formally."

Heavy boots clattered on the stairs from the guard-room.
Julius got up.

"Aaron, thank you, I don't think I'm frightened now.
Will I see you again?"

"I don't know, lad, perhaps not here. God be with you—
but he will be, and I'll pray for you."

Julius bent down and kissed him; then the footsteps came
along the passage and he climbed up in the dim light and
stood just inside the door, waiting.

The door beam rattled back in its sockets and the light
of torches dazzled through as the door swung back. A guard
came in, calling over his shoulder to the other outside. Julius
was invisible in the darkness. The man knocked into him,
throwing him back down the slimy steps. As he fell he cried
one word, a name, then his head hit the stone paving of the
floor.

K

Aaron, in spite of his chains, reached him before the guard. He thrust a hand inside his tunic, and then with great gentleness took the body into his arms.

"I prayed to Him," he whispered. "And He answered."

12

The Wrestler's Cloak

The gates of the legionary fortress of Isca opened with the dawn. The camp lay quiet, waking slowly to a heavy grey mist which hid the sun and held the shadows between the dark barrack blocks. Aemilius stood a little way from the western gate, out of sight of the guards, until he was certain that Con would not come back. The first trumpets were sounding away beyond the Praetorium as the light grew a little stronger. He drew the great folds of his cloak around him, shook the mist dampness from his greying hair and strode off towards the officers' mess and the hope of news, good or evil.

The open ground, past the shuttered stalls to where the first houses loomed through the haze, seemed vast and unfamiliar to Con as he crossed the drawbridge. Not too fast, walking like someone who has an early meeting planned with a friend, not as if he had hardly slept while the dark hours passed and he waited for the guard at the door. He turned as soon as he could among the narrow lanes that led down to the river. Under the curling whiteness of the fog the tide was running high, but perhaps that very fog would give them the time they needed. If only Brychan would not ask the one question that must not be answered yet, not till they were safely out of the town, down river with no way of turning back.

The two cargo barges, flat-bottomed and ugly even in this light, were still there, moored close to the quay below the warehouse. A sailor, swinging his arms to warm himself, came down the gang-plank of the nearest even as Con drew back into the shadows of the gateway. No one else seemed to be stirring, though a scent of wood-smoke drifted from the kitchen behind the merchant's house. The wagon still covered the ladder to the loft. Con climbed it quickly and knelt, peering into the darkness.

There was a movement deep in the shadows. He called softly and Brychan crawled from among the sacks.

Con said, "No, Julius isn't with me, we've got to go on ahead. The boat's still there if we're quick," before the man had time to ask the question that was in his eyes.

Brychan looked dazed still. He moved as far as the edge of the loft and sat down with his feet over the side, shivering a little.

"I brought some food, but there isn't time to eat yet," said Con. "Oh, Brychan, please come, it's nearly high tide, and I can't think of anything else we can do if the boat sails without us."

Brychan shook himself and felt for the first rung of the ladder with his foot. "I'm sorry, Con," he said, as he turned and the boy could see his face again. "It's . . . no, I can't explain now. But Julius?"

"We'll see him later."

At last Brychan seemed to be convinced. He climbed quickly down, and hid behind the wagon while Con peered past him towards the gang-plank of the barge. Not far, hardly twenty paces. He took Brychan's hand and ran; the mist was thinner now and golden up above, there was no time to watch and wait.

Voices came from the bows, and a rancid smell of cooking,

but Con dived down behind the crates and oil jars in the waist of the ship, burrowing deep among them, easing them farther apart to make a place where they could hide. A fold of the canvas cargo cover lay across near the short thick mast. Con reached up to pull it over them, and then froze still as feet ran past on the deck, a voice shouted from the far side and it was jerked out of his hand close above their heads as they crouched in the straw.

Con pulled a corn stalk out of the neck of his tunic and burrowed a place for his feet; then he turned to Brychan in the dim light, unslung the small pack he had carried under his cloak, and handed Brychan the leather drinking bottle.

The boat had reached the estuary, as far as Con could tell from the movement and the sound of the wind in the sail, when at last Brychan spoke. The pale sun was golden now on the canvas above them, and Con, in the cramped space between an oil jar and a basket of apples, had been nearly asleep.

"Julius was taken last night?" the priest asked quietly.

"Yes," Con answered with his eyes half closed, not wanting yet to look at Brychan's face.

"Do you know any more?"

"No."

"But now I've done what you wanted you would tell me the truth if you knew it?"

"Oh, Brychan!" Con caught his breath.

"And your father?"

"He knows. They must have caught Julius almost at once yesterday, thinking he was you. You look alike from a distance, you know; it's mainly the hair, though you are the same height. Father heard about it in the mess, but no one knew who the boy was. Julius hadn't told his name, not last night."

"And not by morning?"

Con twisted the edge of his cloak in his hand till his knuckles were white. He answered in a flat, husky voice. "Father thought they couldn't have questioned him for long last night or they would have come for me by now. Then, when it was nearly morning and everything was still quiet he said I'd better leave Isca with you as soon as I could, while I could still get away. But he wouldn't let me tell him where we were going, in case they question him too."

"Con!"

"But don't you see?" Con looked straight into the eyes of the priest for the first time. "Perhaps we didn't know what we were beginning yesterday. It's too late to think about that now, but I can't keep my mind from what may be happening to Julius this very moment. If he's living through it surely I must be able to talk about it?"

"It may not be very bad for Julius. Could his father not help him?"

"That's what my father asked me, but I don't think Julius would want him to, though he wouldn't be in any danger. It's the same with my father; no one would believe that either of them were Christians. But perhaps neither of them need ever be connected with the arrest of an unknown boy."

"Won't Septimius have missed his son by now?"

"Not with the storm yesterday. He'll think he's with me, and ask my father before he enquires anywhere else. Then he'll tell him . . . whatever there is to tell by then. I don't know what Septimius will do if anything happens to Julius."

They were silent for a while after that. Then Con said, "Brychan, how did it feel when you were in prison? Can you tell me?"

Brychan saw the thought behind Con's question. "I'll try. It was all very strange, not how I'd expected things to be;

you see, you always think of being alone in prison, but really most of the time you are crowded with far too many people, and some of them are noisy and some are ill. Yet in spite of this, when the soldiers put chains on me and took me down to the cells at Caer Taff I was more at peace than I ever remember being before; it was as if the peace was more real than what was going on around me."

"Perhaps that's what Albanus felt."

"I'm sure it must have been. You see, I know what it's like to be frightened, and in one way the fear was still there, only it was being blotted out by something stronger. When I recognised that what I felt was the power of my Master in me I was carried through the next days. I was certain that I was going to die, and the joy that I should soon be with Him was so great that when I was suddenly free yesterday, running through the storm with you, it was as if my strength had suddenly been cut off. I was alone in a darkness that was greater than anything I had known in prison."

"Is everything still dark, Brychan?" asked Con.

The priest stretched out a hand to him. "Do you think I'm so ungrateful?" he said, and there was a hint of a smile in his voice. "No, now I can see that I was like a wrestler who lays by his cloak to free him for a struggle. Now I must take up my cloak and all the difficulties with it, as we all must, and my thoughts keep going back to the others I left behind in Isca, after the days we've been together."

"Perhaps Julius isn't frightened either. But he's not a Christian, is he?" The ache was still in Con's voice.

"Perhaps not as some people would see it. Con, if the worst you fear comes true, there isn't anything I can say that will help you quickly, but will you try to remember one thing and think about it? I may not be with you when the time comes, so I must say it now. There has been so little time when we were together and I couldn't teach you as I would like to have done. You've been caught on the edge of something so big and powerful, you have been sucked in out of your depth. But the one thing I tried to show you was my God's love. It may be difficult to see any love in such pain, but it's a love you must try to believe in, and feel about you, and trust. Julius is part of that love too, and it won't stop for him if he should die. He will have drawn nearer to it, and as you learn more—as I hope you will—you will be coming close to your friend again."

Long cramped hours later, as dusk was falling, they heard the sounds of the barge coming into a harbour going on all around them. When it was quiet again except for the faint watery noises that showed them they were now tied up to some town quay, Con pushed aside the canvas cover and listened cautiously. Far across the rooftops came the sound of a Roman trumpet, lights out at the fort of Caer Taff. Beyond anything they could have hoped they had come home.

All the crew seemed to have gone ashore, and as they crawled out of their hiding place the boat was in darkness except for a lantern in the bows. A maze of small lanes ran up from the quay behind the houses that lined the main road; Con found the one that led to the back of Fabius's stockyard and they picked their way along as far as the oak which Brychan had climbed in the spring. Lights were still burning in the house; the high window of the dining room made a bright square through the branches of the apple trees. They climbed the fence and crouched beside the woodpile.

Con said, "We can't go up to the house until we know that Fabius is there. I'll scout along under the bushes and see if I can see anything."

A projecting corner of the kitchen garden gave him cover most of the way to the terrace. He lay under the currant bushes with the leaves dripping down his neck, where he could see straight through into the atrium. Antonia, the old servant, came out with a pile of dishes and went into the kitchen. Then there was a pause. Con hoped that Brychan was staying where he left him.

The leg of a table scraped on the tiled floor and Domina Helena came to the doorway with Lavinia. They paused, looking out into the garden. Con dropped his head on his arms so that his face would not make a white blur in the darkness.

He was so near that he heard when Domina Helena said, "It's getting cold, these nights. We shall have to start drawing the heavy curtains across the terrace soon."

"But then it will be winter, and it's hardly stopped being summer yet," answered Lavinia. "Mother, have you seen Crumple?"

"No, darling, isn't she in the kitchen?"

A pause. "No, she isn't. Look, she's on your bed."

"Is she though? Yes, Crumple, the idea!"

A tiny furry body streaked past Con.

"I hope she doesn't go too far, it's still very wet out there," said Lavinia.

"Goodnight, darling, don't be too long looking for her." Domina Helena's footsteps moved away.

Con raised his head carefully. Vinny was coming out on to the terrace. She stood for a while silhouetted against the light from the house, and then came slowly down the path between the apple trees.

"Vinny," Con called softly.

She stopped. "Who is it?"

"Me, Con, and Brychan." He slid out of his hiding place. "Come where we can talk."

Vinny followed him down the garden without a word till

she saw Brychan under the tree. Then she gave a little gasp and ran straight into his arms.

"I told myself you were probably dead, but it didn't help," she said, in a voice muffled by his cloak. Brychan sat down, holding her close.

"Sweetheart," he asked, "is your father here?"

"No, he went away yesterday to Isca, he won't be back till tomorrow."

"Then I must go out into the woods for the night, and then westward when we see how the hunt goes," he said, and there was great weariness in his voice.

"Oh, I see," said Vinny. "Did you want somewhere to hide? But there's the store-room next to my bedroom. No one ever goes there."

"Not without your father here, Vinny. You don't understand how dangerous it would be." Brychan's voice sounded final.

"I do, Father told me, when I asked what had happened to you. He told me about being a Christian, and I know he'd want you to hide here, that's why he went to Isca. Mother would too."

"Your mother would see me as a danger come into her house and near her children and she would be right."

"Then Mother needn't know."

"Vinny," said Con, "think carefully. Would it really work? Isn't that store-room over where Antonia sleeps? She'd hear if anyone started moving above her."

"No, she wouldn't. Antonia's deaf as a post, and anyway she spends most of the time by the kitchen fire when she isn't asleep. As long as Brychan didn't walk about in the middle of the night it would be all right, and I could easily get food. Brychan, please stay—till Father comes home anyway."

"There's nothing else you can do. You can't get across the bridge tonight, and it will only be for a day," said Con.

"And what will you do now?" asked Brychan doubtfully.

"I'll go home," said Con. "It's too late for anything else. I can tell my mother I came home because I wasn't well."

"Vinny, how can I get into the house?" asked Brychan.

"I'll go back now. When Mother and the others have gone to bed, I'll wave something white from my window; look, you can see it over the roof. The stairs are at the end of the atrium on the left. I must go now or Mother will think I've been kidnapped." They heard her calling her cat among the trees.

"She's a good child," said Brychan.

Con sat down wearily and pulled his damp cloak round him. They waited in silence under the dripping branches of the tree, watching the lights in the house go out one by one.

"It won't be long now," said Con. "I wonder if I shall ever see you again."

Brychan roused himself. The moon was rising and they could see each other's faces a little more clearly. "I don't know, Con. This summer I thought I could see so far ahead. My bishop had given me work to do and I had my plans in my head as a gardener has when he's decided on his spring sowing."

"But haven't you been saved from Clodius Priscus so you can do it all still?"

"Perhaps so, I don't know. There may be things I still need to learn before I can serve in that way."

"What things?"

"I don't know yet. Patience perhaps, and the kind of trust you showed yesterday, both of you, when you opened the door of my prison."

Con's tired mind began to wander backwards through the

last hours, too close to see the pattern which was almost under his feet, glad that Fabius would soon be home and Brychan would pass into his keeping. Perhaps his father would send word by him tomorrow from Isca and the pain of ignorance at least would be eased. And by now whatever the day had held for his friend would be over one way or another. He looked back towards the house.

"Look, there's Vinny. Brychan, you must go."

"Very well. But one thing, from now on you must do nothing more to put yourself in danger. I don't like the risk I shall be to Fabius, but that doesn't alter the fact that you have done enough. We must not meet again, and you must not come to this house till you hear from Fabius that it's safe to do so."

"I suppose not," said Con unwillingly. "And I don't know what more I could do. Goodbye, Brychan, for however long it must be. Will you bless me like you did once before? It was Julius who understood things better, but now I've got to try to understand by myself."

He dropped on his knees in the darkness, and Brychan placed his hands on the bowed head and blessed him with words that were unfamiliar but full of hope. Then, before Con realised it, he was gone through the shadows of the wet garden towards the darkened house.

13

Night in Caer Taff

Lavinia woke with a start. There were men talking loudly outside in the road, although it still felt very early. Then she remembered Brychan. There was no curtain at the little front window and she looked out into the street. In the half light a centurion and two soldiers were examining a loaded wagon that had just come up from the harbour. As she watched, other men came out of a house farther down the road and knocked on the shutters of their neighbour's shop.

She froze back against the wall as one glanced up at her window. It looked as if the whole town was being searched, and Mother did not even know that Brychan was in the house. Even as she realised this, there was a heavy knock on their own door; it was too late to do anything now. She got back into bed and pulled the clothes up around her.

It was some time before they made old Antonia hear, and after that she heard her mother's voice, very cool and annoyed.

"But this is ridiculous. My husband is away and there's no one here except my children and my servants. By what right do you search my house?"

It sounded as if the soldiers had sent for a more senior officer, for there was an uneasy pause. Then she said, "Very well, Centurion, if you must; but I must beg you not to frighten my children."

The men were in the atrium now. It did not sound from the opening and shutting of doors as if they were searching very carefully. Then there were footsteps on the stairs. Lavinia clenched her hands under the blankets; she knew she was looking frightened, she only hoped that the guilt did not show as well. Her mother opened the door.

"I'm sorry to disturb you, Lavinia, but it seems the house must be searched for some escaped prisoner." She came over to the bed, sitting down with her arm around the child.

It was the Centurion himself who came in next. He stood, very large and out of place among the trappings of a small girl's room, and looked around him in silence. There was nowhere for even a child to hide. He made a token swipe under the bed with his cane and was turning to go when he noticed the door of the store-room. To her horror Vinny saw that it was a little open.

"What's in there?" he asked.

"It's only a store," said Domina Helena. "No one could get in there with the child asleep in bed. That is the only door."

"Better have a look all the same." But as he walked over to it, swinging his cane, it moved a little wider of itself, and Crumple stalked out with her tail erect and an air of complete unconcern.

All at once she saw the man, stopped dead with one paw still raised, and then streaked for the open window which led to the sloping roof of the atrium and the safety of the garden. At the far side of the lightwell she paused to look back, saw the soldiers below, and skidded out of sight.

"Well," said the man. "What a funny little beast! She certainly doesn't like strangers. No need to look in that room

now. Thank you, madam, and I'm sorry I had to disturb you." He clanked down the stairs.

"It's all right, darling, don't be frightened, it's all over now. I'll come back in a minute." Domina Helena hurried after him. Below, across the courtyard, little Lesbius began to wail dolefully.

Lavinia began to cry herself, but with relief. She was back in bed with the door shut by the time her mother came upstairs with a cup of warm milk.

"But, Mother," said Vinny, hiccuping into it, "what would have happened if they'd found anybody?"

"They'd have taken him away, of course. But don't worry about it, we don't know who it was; still, I wish your father had been here. Do you think you could go back to sleep, it's still very early?"

Lavinia lay down and let her mother tuck her up. A little while after she had gone, the store-room door opened again quietly and Brychan came out. He sat down on the bed where Domina Helena had been a few minutes before, and smiled at Lavinia.

"So the little cat knows her friends after all! She found me at midnight and she's been asleep in the crook of my arm ever since. It was she who woke me just now, not the guard, for I was sleeping sounder than I have for months."

"Dear Crumple, I'm glad she's done one useful thing in her whole life," said Lavinia.

Fabius did not come back till late in the afternoon. As soon as her mother was safely in the kitchen Lavinia sent her little brother down the garden on an errand and followed her father into his room.

"Please can you come upstairs with me now? It's particularly important."

Fabius did not look up from the saddle bag he was unpacking; he seemed more tired than usual after a journey, and worried. "Can it wait till we've eaten, Vinny?"

"Father?"

Something in her voice made him turn to look at her. "Oh, I see, it means that much, does it?"

Vinny nodded her head, speechless, and took him up the narrow stairs. Once inside the small bedroom she opened the door to the store-room and stood back. Brychan got up from the chest where he had been sitting and the two men met in the centre of the room. As Fabius caught Brychan by the shoulders Vinny slipped quietly away, shutting the door behind her, and sat down at the turn of the stair to keep guard.

She heard her father's voice, and then Brychan speaking very urgently, then silence. Very soon the door opened quickly and Fabius nearly fell over her in the darkness on the stairs. He knelt down beside her, holding her very close, and kissed her hair.

"Vinny, you've been so brave, just one more thing," he said. "When it's dark I'm going to take Brychan away. Now I must go and tell your mother all that's been happening, but will you go down to the stockyard and find Probus for me? There's a message I must get to Con that I daren't write down or trust to Probus alone, but he can go with you to Aemilius's house and then you can tell Con yourself. Can you do that?"

"Yes, of course I can. What shall I say?"

"Tell Con I'm home, and that Brychan will be safe across the river tonight. I'll come to him then if I can, even if it's nearly morning. He must stay awake and watch for me. I'll go past the front of the house so that he can hear me, and then he can let me in through the garden gate."

"How will he know it's you?"

"It's a good thing you thought of that. Tell Con I'll cough

L   161

several times as I go past, then he can go and unfasten the gate. That's the best thing I can think of now. I hope there aren't too many men in Caer Taff tonight with colds!"

"I'll tell him," said Vinny.

She went quickly into her room to fetch a cloak. Brychan was standing well back from the window looking westwards through the fading light. He did not speak, and she watched him a moment, suddenly timid; only the knowledge that when she came back he might be gone, made her go up and touch his arm.

"What is it, sweetheart?" Then he looked down at her. "Yes, this will be goodbye again. I was looking at the woods over there, coloured like fire, and it was only in spring when the leaves were first green that I came into this house for the first time."

"Another summer, or even next spring and you'll be back again, I know you will—if you want to see us after so many terrible things have happened to you here."

His arm stiffened under her hand, then relaxed again. "If ever the time comes when I can walk the road freely again, I'll come."

She stood on tiptoe to kiss him and then ran quickly out of the room. Below, the door of her mother's room was shut and she thought she could hear weeping, but there was no time to stop now.

Long, dark hours later Con sat upright with a jerk. His head had nodded back against the atrium wall. He pulled the blanket closer round his shoulders, feeling the cold from the stone bench working more deeply into his bones. No, this time there really were footsteps on the road outside. They slowed, stopped, started again, and there was the sound of coughing, and for good measure a nose being blown as well.

Con threw the blanket down and reached for the lamp he

had set ready. Shielding the tiny flame in his hand, he hurried out and along the narrow path that led through an untidy hedge to the vegetable plot and the back gate. Fabius was already there as he swung it open.

The architect stepped quickly through and then leaned against the wall, nearly asleep on his feet.

"The gardener's shed," said Con. "We can't talk in the house."

He led the tired man to the little lean-to built against the back wall. Fabius sat down on an upturned basket and looked up at Con, uncertain where to begin.

"Wait a minute," said Con, "I won't be long."

He left the lamp on the shelf and ran quickly up the familiar paths towards the house. The darkness seemed less complete now, although the moon had set, it must be coming towards dawn. Almost at once he was back with the blanket and a jug of wine. Fabius drank thirstily while Con tucked the cover round him.

After a while the warmth and the wine seemed to have their effect and Fabius smiled. "I didn't see how we could manage it, Con, but he's safe. We crossed the river a mile above the fort. Winter's coming on and there are days of hiding in the woods ahead, but somehow I'm sure that now he's alone Brychan won't be taken again."

"Oh, Fabius, we won."

"Yes, I suppose so. It was a little like a battle, wasn't it?" Fabius stopped suddenly, looking at Con.

"You came from Isca, didn't you?" Con said gently. "Tell me, Fabius, it can't be more horrible than the things I've been thinking these last hours."

"It wasn't quite the worst, Con, but Julius is dead. That was what you were expecting, wasn't it?"

Con turned away, standing with his hands on the two

sides of the doorway, his head bowed. Then he looked up, westward, where the sky was still dark, and said without turning, "How did it happen?"

Fabius told him all that Aemilius had been able to find out that morning in Isca, and what he had been able to guess. When he had finished Con asked, "Is Father safe now?"

"Yes, of course. When Julius died he still hadn't told his name; there was nothing to connect him with you or Aemilius. In a place the size of Isca your sudden departure wasn't noticed."

"Does Septimius know yet?"

"Yes, your father went to him as soon as he heard the rumour of Julius's death. In all my life there has never been a task I was more thankful to see done by someone else. Your father said he seemed stunned, like a man after a fall. He won't be the man he was this summer again."

"Will he come back now?"

"Yes, today or tomorrow, and I think your father will be with him. Septimius is in no state to travel alone."

Con turned at last and looked at Fabius, and the architect saw that he was still dry-eyed. "I don't think I could ever see Septimius again."

"Perhaps not yet. This is his tragedy. Not ours, or even Julius's, whatever we may think. Julius is safe, if the Christians are to be believed, Brychan is free, and the rest of us . . ."

"We're caught up in the undertow. Brychan said once that the spreading of his faith was like the waves of the spring tide advancing up the beach. We've been caught up in the water and set down we don't know where, and most of us alone. Brychan is alone, and Fabius, will I ever know anyone as well as I knew Julius?" At last Con was crying.

Fabius stood up and put an arm round the boy, not trying to stop the tears, till Con gulped and was quiet again.

"You must go," he said. "I can't think how to explain to Mother that Father may be back today, so I'll have to leave it to Father to tell her what he thinks best when he comes."

"Goodbye for now, Con," said Fabius. "If you can, try to sleep, it does help. Perhaps later you'll come round and talk to Vinny. She doesn't know about Julius yet and I must tell her, but I think you two could perhaps be more use to each other than I am."

"Dear Vinny, she's helped so much. Yes, I'll come."

Con shut the gate behind Fabius, picked up the blanket and blew out the lamp. Birds were waking in the garden as he walked slowly back towards the house. His room was cool and grey, unfamiliar. He sat down automatically to undress, but before he had finished a dark tide of unconsciousness began to flow over him. The blanket was ready and he covered himself as his eyes closed.

14

The Emperor's Standards

Autumn was nearly over. The chestnuts which a month ago had turned red in one night were bare, and the yellow beech leaves that had shone like a shower of gold in the thickets lay trodden into the mud beside the faded amber and pink woodland grass. Con made the last calculated blow with his axe and an apple tree in Fabius's garden, older than the house itself, tottered over on to its side in a welter of dirty black twigs and the last of the wizened apples that had been too high to reach.

Vinny's face appeared on the far side of the bush of branches. "Hullo, I kept away until it was down. I wasn't sure you really knew where it would go, in spite of what you said."

Con walked round to see how the tree lay. "I wasn't certain myself, but I got it right for all that. Straight between the two pippins, with no bark off either!"

"Con, do you wonder sometimes how you ever had time to go to school?" asked Vinny.

"Yes, I know what you mean." Con wiped the blade of his axe on the skirt of his disreputable tunic and put it down. "And Vinny, if this summer had been an ordinary one I should have been at school now."

"So you would. Con, everything that's happened hasn't

changed things very much for me, but how much longer will you go on being busy and doing nothing?"

"I don't know," said Con. "If anyone had told me this time last year that by now I wouldn't even want to join the Legion I should have thought they were mad, but it's true, as things are I don't."

"Con, are you really sure of that? Honestly, if someone said, 'You needn't sacrifice to the Emperor and you're never going to have to hunt down Christians,' wouldn't you be glad?"

Con looked down at his dirty sandals, wondering how to explain the emotions he could not control or comprehend himself to this little, dark-haired girl who during the last months had seemed to understand him so well.

"Of course I should. I should run straight down the road to Isca just as I am! But that's not how life in the Legion would be for me now. If Brychan had been here I think we should have become Christians; without him it's more than I can do on my own. But I can see anyway that the army isn't now and perhaps never was what I thought it. I can't see what I'm going to do at the moment, and there doesn't seem much point in looking ahead. We've already seen how the future can change in a single night. I can feel inside me that this isn't the time for making plans."

"So meanwhile you cut down trees for my father, and build a new wall at the bottom of your own garden, and play with Lesbius."

"Building walls and playing with children may be ordinary, unexciting things, but they're surprisingly comforting. At the moment I don't even want to do anything else."

"And what about your father?"

"I think he's changed as much as I have. He seemed almost glad when I told him I didn't want to be a soldier

167

any more, and I didn't have to explain why to him because he feels the same way himself. Did you know how alike we are? I hadn't understood till now. It's worse for him, though, because the army's been his life and he must look backwards at things he can't change, instead of forward as I do."

Con walked up and down, suddenly restless. Vinny said nothing, watching and wondering. Con turned on his heel and asked, "Has your father seen Septimius lately?"

"Yes, two days ago. Poor man, he still doesn't leave his house."

"Have you noticed," said Con, "that our fathers seem more changed than we are? It's as if things they thought they were sure of have suddenly shifted under them. It's not only what we did, it's everything that's happened these last months all over the Empire."

"Yes, it seems to be harder for grown-ups to change than it is for us," said Vinny. "I suppose they get out of practice."

"That's a wise thought! Jupiter, it's getting dark already, how short the afternoons are. I'll have to come tomorrow and clear up." Con collected his tools together. "Hey, look, here's Lesbius."

The little boy was running towards them as fast as he could along a twisting path under the bare trees that was known only to himself. Con caught him up and swung him high; the child's face was sticky and he was only wearing his indoor tunic.

"Well, Lesbius, are you running away or were you trying to find us? Have you been bothering Antonia again?"

"No, Con. Put me down." He wriggled till the boy set him on his feet. "Father says will you come. First there was a man on a horse. He rode straight in through the gate, I saw him, and the horse was all dirty. Then Father came back and he hadn't even combed his hair after his bath, and now he says you're to come."

"Where is he then? You show us." Con took him by the hand and they walked back together to the house.

The architect was pacing up and down in the atrium, still wearing his cloak, while Domina Helena stood still, looking on helplessly. When she saw them she said, "Now, perhaps you'll tell us what's happened. You're worse than Lesbius!"

"It's this. A messenger rode in less than an hour ago, I was at the bath-house and I heard the news as soon as anyone. It's happened, Helena, what we've longed for for years. We have one Empire again, the division is over. At last there's one man in charge who's big enough to rule all of us as we were ruled in the old days."

"But which man?" asked Domina Helena, still perplexed.

"Constantine, of course. The armies met at last in Italy. It had to be there, nowhere else is final enough to decide the fate of the Empire. There was a battle at a place called the Milvian Bridge and Maxentius was routed. That's all I know except for one thing."

"And what's that?" asked Con.

"It seems that the Legions of Constantine went into battle under strange standards. Oh, I expect the Eagles were there, but at the last moment the Emperor, your namesake, Con, ordered that other ones should be made as well. They were like this." He dipped a finger in the pool and drew a simple sign on the tiled surround.

Vinny looked over his shoulder. "It's the Greek letters Khi and Rho written on top of each other. But, Father, that's a Christian sign. It's a short way of writing the name of God; Brychan showed it to me."

"Just so. It seems that the Emperor had a dream that in that sign he would triumph. He believed it and he was right."

"His mother was a Christian, wasn't she, or that's what we've always heard," said Con.

"Yes, and she's British too." Domina Helena came to her husband's side. "But what does this mean to us, both the new Emperor, and the Christian sign?"

"Security I think, for one thing. A garrison in Isca that's up to strength, not split with some cohorts fighting other Romans in Gaul, and a few men trying to hold down this frontier. That will be good, but the other thing is even more important. It means an end to the persecution; that much is clear already."

"So if this had happened last year Brychan would never have been arrested and everything would have been all right, and now he can come back," said Vinny. "Father, do you know where he is? Can you go and get him?"

"It's not as easy as that," said Fabius. "We must be quite sure first." Suddenly he stretched his arms wide and smiled.

"Oh, but it's a good feeling, it's like the beginning of spring, not the end of autumn."

"You know, sir, it couldn't all have happened in the spring," said Con thoughtfully. "It would have been too early in the year to mount a big campaign. The big battles are always fought at the beginning of winter when no one can waste any more time and things have to be decided at once."

Fabius started to laugh. "Con, for two months you've assured everyone that you wouldn't join the Eagles if you could, and now listen to you!"

Con blushed. "Who says I'm going to now? But I can't help the way my mind works. I must go, it's almost dark and I don't know if Father will have heard the news yet, he's at home today. Domina Helena, I'm sorry I'm leaving your garden in such a mess; I'll come tomorrow and get the tree cut up."

Fabius went with him to the door and Lavinia followed them. "But, Father, when will Brychan come back?" She put her hand into his.

"You never think of more than one thing at a time, do you?" He laughed. "The Empire could have collapsed and it would have been all the same to you if you could see your friend again."

"Anyone would think you didn't want to see him too," she said primly.

"I want that almost more than anything else in the world, I think," he said, not speaking to her any longer. "Yet we must be sure. I want Brychan at my table freely, as my friend. I want Helena to know him better and really understand at last what it is he can bring us; I want him to teach my children. I've lain in the dark these nights and been hungry for these things as I haven't known hunger since I was a boy. It's no wonder it seems spring to me."

"Spring tide," said Con, turning in the doorway. "I remember, it seems as if Brychan's last small wave has been added and now the tide is in flood and has washed everything before it. I wonder what the wave was."

"Perhaps it was something the Emperor's mother did or said when he was a small child, or something he heard later that lay in the back of his mind and that grew and changed him without his knowing it. Think, Con, all those days' journey away in Italy; now what the Emperor dreamed a month ago has changed our lives, here at the edge of the world. And you will be a better soldier, I think, because this happened to you first."

"Why, what do you mean?"

"Before, it was mainly that you wanted to do what would please your father, and to be like him. Now you will want and understand the thing itself."

"I suppose you're right. I don't know how it will work out with being a Christian though, even now. I shall have to ask Brychan about that. It's funny, we all seem quite certain that he will be allowed to come back to us."

To the west across the bridge lay the darkening countryside with the road still a pale ribbon between the shadows of the woods. "I remember the first time I saw him," said Con. "Out there on the road. I wonder when he will come back again, the same young man with red hair, but coming alone this time, and knowing what his welcome will be."

"Perhaps not till spring. The roads are bad already and we don't know how far away he may be."

"But early next summer I must leave for Isca! Oh, if only Julius could have been here now." At last he had said what had been in his mind from the moment Fabius had told them of the end of the persecution. He turned his head away. "He seems a long way away already. Almost nobody talks about him any more, either because they're afraid or because it hurts too much. Before long his death and Aaron's will be forgotten, and why it was they died."

"That might happen," said Fabius, "though their names may live far longer than we can imagine, even after people have forgotten what they were like. Yet, while you remember Julius he's still a part of you, Con, and I think what Brychan can teach us will bring him even closer."

"If Brychan's God can really do that it won't be hard to believe in him."

"Listen to the evening trumpets," said Vinny. "They're sounding for a new Emperor!"

"And a new Empire," whispered Fabius.

"Blessed Alban the inhabitant of Verulamium," wrote the monk Gildas, three hundred years later, "Aaron and Julius of the City of the Legions, and moreover others of both sexes, pressed on, in their different ways, in the forefront of the battle line of Christ."